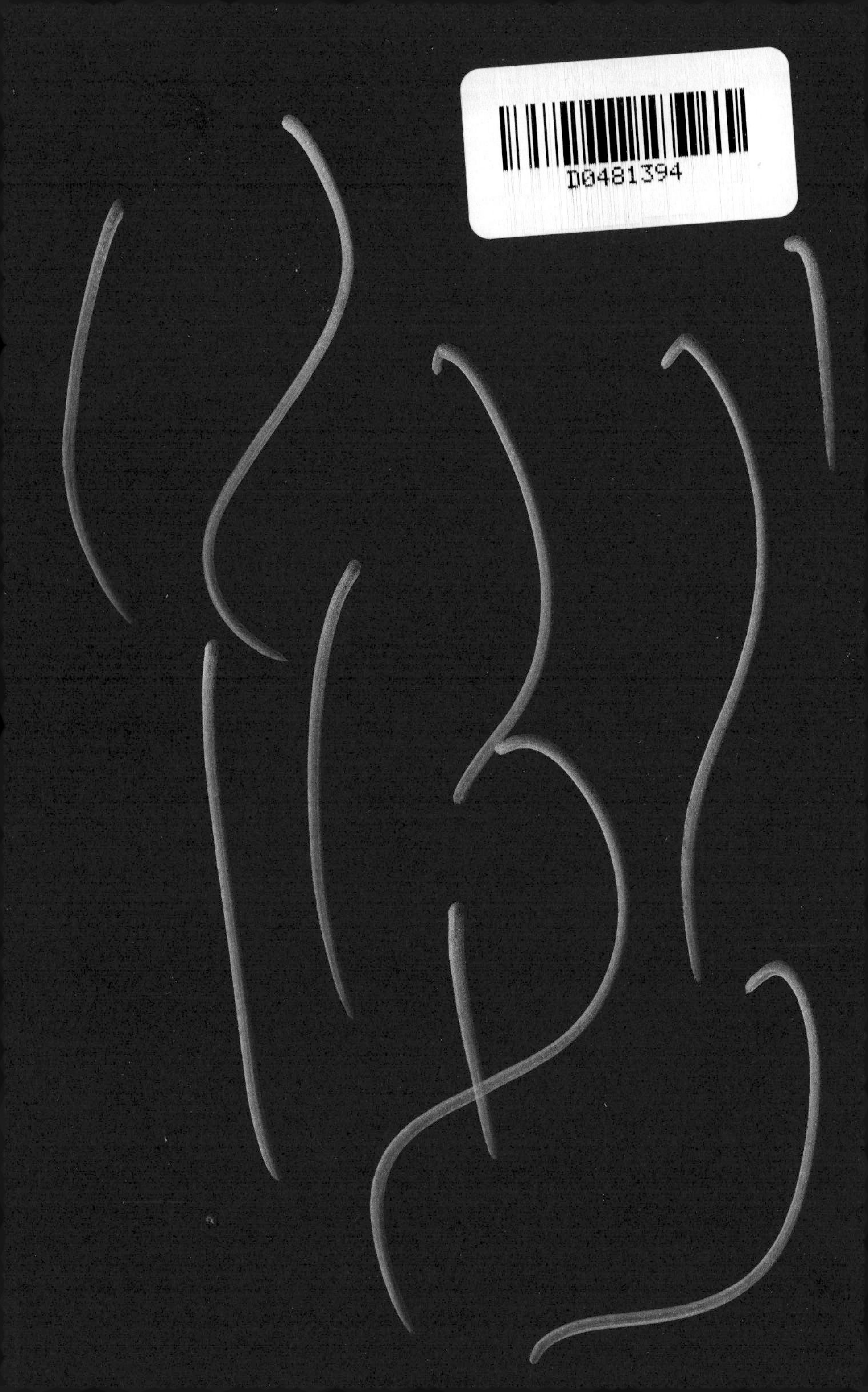

SCHOLASTIC PRESS
NEW YORK

FOR
MICHELLE
DURAN

LIBRARY OF CONGRESS CATALOGING-IN-PUBLICATION DATA

Names: Avi, 1937- author.
Title: City of magic / Avi. Description: First edition. | New York: Scholastic Press, 2022. | Companion book to: Midnight magic and Murder at midnight. | Audience: Ages 8–12. | Audience: Grades 4–6. | Summary: Mangus the Magician and his thirteen-year-old servant, Fabrizio, are commanded to go to Venice, on pain of death, to find a book by Friar Luca Pacioli that reportedly contains a magical means of making money; but Venice is a strange and dangerous city, and someone else is also after the book—then Mangus is arrested, and taken to the prison, and Fabrizio and Bianca, an orphan he has met, must find a way to secure the book, save Mangus, and themselves.
Identifiers: LCCN 2021018695 | ISBN 9780545321976 (hardcover)
Subjects: LCSH: Magicians—Juvenile fiction. | Orphans—Juvenile fiction. | Magic tricks—Juvenile fiction. | Renaissance—Italy—Venice—Juvenile fiction. | Adventure stories. | Venice (Italy)—History—15th century—Juvenile fiction. | CYAC: Magicians—Fiction. | Magic tricks—Fiction. | Orphans—Fiction. | Adventure and adventurers—Fiction. | Renaissance—Italy—Venice—Fiction. | Venice (Italy)—History—15th century—Fiction. | Italy—History—15th century—Fiction. | LCGFT: Action and adventure fiction. | Historical fiction.
Classification: LCC PZ7.A953 Ci 2022 | DDC 813.54 [Fic]—dc23

10 9 8 7 6 5 4 3 2 1 22 23 24 25 26

Printed in the U.S.A. 37

First edition, June 2022

Book design by Marijka Kostiw

PERGAMONTIO, ITALY
MARCH 1492

CHAPTER 1

HERE COMES TROUBLE!

That was my first thought when the horse and carriage stopped in front of our house.

But, with permission, I must begin by telling you my name is Fabrizio, and I am the thirteen-year-old servant of Mangus the Magician. That morning, I'd been doing one of my many chores — sweeping the hall — and had opened the front door to brush out the dust and let in the morning sun. So it was me who saw the carriage arrive with its team of horses. Painted on the carriage door was the crest of Pergamontio's king, Claudio the Thirteenth. Whenever *that* carriage with *that* sign came to our house, it always brought disaster.

No sooner did the carriage stop than a man leaped out.

He was a tall, sharp-faced man, with a pointy nose, thin lips, bright eyes, and a spiky red beard. His shimmering green silk jacket reached his knees. On his legs were multi-colored leggings and fine leather boots. A flat black cap sat on his head. Sticking up from that cap was a peacock feather whose vanes came together in the shape of a blue-green eye that seemed to glare at me with anger. But what made me truly uneasy was the dagger that hung from his belt, its blade so sharp it glittered.

All that said, Master and Mistress insisted that whenever anyone came to our door — beggar or baron — I must greet them with courtesy. I, therefore, dropped my straw broom, hurried forward, and bowed.

"Signore," I said, "with permission, how may I be of service?"

The man barked back: "I am Signor Lorenzo Rozetti, Pergamontio's royal tax collector, in the service of King Claudio. In the person of me, he commands Mangus the Magician to attend him immediately."

Mangus was called "the Magician" because he had performed magic shows in Pergamontio for many years even though he refused to admit he knew *any* true wizardry. Then King Claudio forbade the performances. So whenever my master's name — Mangus — was linked to the word *magic*, I was instructed to say, as I did: "Signore, my master no longer performs magic."

But I do, I reminded myself, not that I was about to admit it.

"I don't give a fig what Mangus does," returned Signor Rozetti in an arrogant voice. "The king commands he come at once."

Trying to hide my alarm, I said, "Yes, Signore, of course. Absolutely. I'll tell my master right away."

I started to go, but being worried, I stopped and turned back. "Signore, with permission, may I tell my master something more?"

"Advise him," said the tax collector, putting a hand to his dagger's hilt, "that he might not return home."

Truly frightened, I slammed the door shut, bolted it, and raced down the hallway to where my master was.

Mangus's study looked the way a magician's room should look. Below a low, soot-blackened oak-beamed ceiling, everything was shadowy and still. Only a few fingers of light slipped through the solitary window's splintered shutter, lighting up motes of dust that swirled through the gloom like stars in a midnight sky.

On the floor, a firepot offered no heat, just ashes.

Against the walls, sagging shelves were stuffed with battered books and musty manuscripts. Many of the volumes were about magic, charms, and omens. Though I was forbidden to read those books, you may be sure I did — in secret. Of late, I'd been studying omens, which allowed me to foresee the future.

Many a midnight I heard the old man's feather pen scrape and scratch like a scurrying rat, which convinced me he was writing mystic incantations. But when I asked him what he had been composing, all he would say was "Philosophy."

I didn't believe him.

In the room's center stood a heavy oak table, on which a human skull had been placed. (I had no idea whose.) In the empty head was a thick candle, placed so that light could shine through the hollow eye sockets and brighten any pages that lay before Mangus. That morning, the candle had become as lifeless as the skull: a most regrettable omen. Moreover, Master had fallen asleep over his writing, another unlucky sign.

As for Mangus, he was a short, stoop-shouldered, and

sad-eyed old man, with a much-wrinkled face from which dangled a frowsy gray beard that looked like a tattered paintbrush. On his head was a leather cap with flaps that covered his few strands of gray hair as well as his large, hairy ears. Draped over his back was a dark wool cape, while on his feet were boots of moth-eaten rabbit fur.

What you need to know is that I had come to live with Mangus and his wife, Mistress Sophia, two years before. I had been a homeless street orphan, and they brought me into their home so I might take care of them and their house. So I cleaned, ran errands, and fetched what they needed. In return, they fed me and gave me a straw bed in their tiny attic. I am happy to acknowledge they treated me kindly. Moreover, in such free time as I had, I did as I wished. To be sure, I had no money, but I was content.

That said, my sole complaint was that the old man *refused* to teach me any magic. He claimed he didn't know any. How exasperating. How annoying. How regrettable. If I'd known even a bit of magic, I would have done all manner of marvelous things.

In truth, my great fear was that the old man might die

without passing on any of his secrets to me. If that happened, I'd become what I had been before: an orphan beggar on Pergamontio's streets. You may be sure, then, beyond all else, I needed to keep Mangus alive.

I touched the old man's arm and said, "With permission, Master. You must get up."

Stiff from sleeping in an awkward position, Mangus sat slowly and rubbed his wrinkled face with half-mittened hands. He pulled at his beard and yawned.

(This worried me because as I had learned in one of his books, if you don't cover your mouth when you yawn, evil spirits can slip into your body.)

"Is it . . . is it already morning, Fabrizio?" Mangus asked in his scratchy voice.

Knowing the king's summons would upset him, I was reluctant to speak.

Mangus turned to look at me. I was wearing my patched tunic with a frayed rope belt around my waist and cloth boots on my feet. My thick black hair was — as always — a snarl. But I suppose the only thing Mangus noticed was my dark eyes, my stub nose, my olive complexion, and my round face, which at that moment I'm sure was full of worry.

"Has something unpleasant happened, Fabrizio?"

"Forgive me, Master," I replied. "A gentleman is asking for Mangus the Magician."

"Tell him to go away," muttered the old man, and he leaned back over the table and cradled his head in his arms.

I gave him another gentle poke. "It's the royal tax collector, Master. Sent by King Claudio."

"Why should the king send him?" muttered Mangus. "I have no money."

"All he would tell me is that you might not return home."

Those ominous words made Mangus pop up so fast it caused him to wince. His face had turned paler than usual. "Fabrizio, did he truly say such an appalling thing?"

"Master, I know it's better to have no answer than a bad one, and I did ask for more facts, but that's all the signore would say. Though it's unpleasant, I'm afraid you must go. With permission, I'll be at your side."

"Ah, Fabrizio, the more you hurry, the shorter your life."

"Forgive me, Master, people say that the shorter the

life, the greater the need to hurry. Perhaps you should use your magic to make yourself disappear."

"Fabrizio, you know I've nothing to do with magic."

"Master, magic is the best way to make people respect you."

"Nonsense."

"If the world makes no sense, Master, nonsense must do."

The old man smiled. "Fabrizio, if the devil appeared, you would joke with him."

"Alas, Master, I fear that the devil is already at our door."

Mangus's good humor faded. His sad gray eyes filled with anxiety. "Did the king truly ask that I come?"

"Not *ask*, Master. Command."

"Then I have no choice," Mangus said with a sigh. With that, he set his hands on the chair armrests and pushed himself into a standing position. Once up, he wobbled, but when I reached out to steady him, he waved me away.

"Master, I'll go with you to the king. Shall I tell Mistress we're leaving?"

The lines on Mangus's face deepened. "Yes, go tell her. The least I can do is say farewell to my good wife."

With that, I tore from Master's study to the bedroom on the second floor. When I got there, Mistress Sophia was already awake and fastening her robe.

She was a slight, white-haired woman whose kindness toward me meant my affection for her was great. But alas, over time she, too, had become frail. It was hard enough to tend to the old man: Taking care of two old people was four times more difficult.

"Fabrizio," she said. "I heard voices. It's early for callers. Is something the matter?"

"Mistress, I'm afraid King Claudio has commanded Master to come to the Castello."

"Why?" she cried.

"The king didn't send reasons, Mistress, just an unpleasant man. And the nasty fellow said Master might not return."

"Dearest Saint Monica," sighed Sophia, and she crossed herself. "Fabrizio, you must go with Mangus and protect him. No, wait." She opened a small ivory casket and took out some Pergamontio coins and closed my fingers over them. "You may need these."

"It's true, Mistress," I said. "Money opens more locks than keys." I put the coins in my pocket but held one back. Using my thumb and index finger, I placed the coin in the palm of my left hand and then curled the fingers of my left hand over the coin, hiding it. Next, I stuck three fingers of my right hand — and my thumb — beneath the curled left fingers, over the coin. Using my right-hand thumb, I slid the coin into my right palm and took away my left hand. When I opened that hand, it appeared as if the coin had vanished.

"Fabrizio," Sophia scolded with a smile, "this is no time for pretend magic."

"Mistress, I learned it from one of Master's books."

"And how many times have we told you not to do such tricks? People believe it's real magic."

"But when I do magic, Mistress, I gain respect," I said, and gave her a loving hug.

She ran a hand through my hair to make it less messy. "Fabrizio, I worry what will become of you."

"Don't worry, Mistress. I intend to become the world's greatest magician. May I have some bread?"

"Why?"

"One of Master's books says that if you put a piece of bread in your pocket, you'll have good luck. Besides, I'm hungry."

"Foolish boy," Mistress Sophia called as I rushed down the steps and found my agitated master, who was pacing the hallway. Within moments, Mistress Sophia joined us, and I stood aside as they spoke loving farewells.

There was pounding on the door. I peeked out. It was that awful man, the one with the feather in his cap and the dagger on his hip.

"Master," I called, "we must go."

"I'm ready," Mangus said in a voice that suggested the opposite.

We were about to step outside when Mistress Sophia held me back. As she handed me a loaf of bread, she whispered, "Fabrizio, stay close to him. He needs protection."

"With my life, Mistress."

"And no magic tricks," she added. "They only cause trouble."

"Understood, Mistress," I said, guiding my master out the door even as I wondered if we would ever come back.

CHAPTER 2

LEANING ON MY ARM, MANGUS STEPPED ONTO THE ancient cobblestone street and moved toward the king's carriage, whose door hung open like a hungry mouth. The tax collector was standing there waiting, a smirk on his lips, a hand on his dagger.

As I helped Mangus climb into the carriage and then followed, I thought, *I need to put this arrogant tax collector in his place.*

The door slammed behind us. To my relief, the tax collector sat up by the driver. With the snap of a whip, the carriage lurched into motion.

Inside the dismal, cold cab, Mangus and I sat facing each other, our knees bumping. Seeing that he looked like wretchedness itself, I tore off a bit of bread and shoved it into my pocket — for luck — then offered a larger piece to Mangus.

"Thank you," the old man said. His knotty hand was trembling, and he never did put the bread into his mouth.

"Master," I said, keeping my voice low so that the tax

collector couldn't hear, "have no worries. I'll take good care of you."

"That," growled Mangus, "is what the flea said when he jumped on the bear's back."

"But, Master, as people say, an itch can remind you that you're alive. Have you any idea what's so urgent?"

"For the rich and powerful," said Mangus, "everything in life is urgent."

"For the poor and weak, Master, nothing is urgent but life. Do you think your life is in danger?"

"Fabrizio, it's my soul I must protect."

"Have no fear, Master; I put bread in my pocket for good luck."

"Ignorant superstition," growled Mangus. "Now, stop your prattle. I must think about what I might have done to offend the king. And what might be my punishment," he added before folding his hands together and closing his eyes.

I knew that magic would make such troubles as we were now facing so much easier to handle. But once again I was frustrated by Mangus's refusal to admit he knew any. I sat back, wishing in vain there was something I could do about it. Meanwhile, the swaying, jostling carriage sped up Pergamontio's narrow, steep streets, where, as usual, few were about. We crossed the town's low, listless river, kept going, and soon reached the city summit, where we halted.

When we did, the carriage door was yanked open. I looked out. We had come to the king's gloomy Castello, which was topped by turrets and a crenellated wall where metal-helmeted sentries paced.

Be ready to defend Master, I told myself as I helped him step out. The bread was left behind.

Once alighted, Mangus was shoved forward by Signor Rozetti, which caused my anger toward the tax collector to increase.

We walked over a bridge that crossed a deep moat and then mounted steps, blocked by a heavy gate. A password was called for and returned by Rozetti — "King Claudio is kind!" The gate opened.

A covered walkway led to a long gallery, at the end of which was a closed door. Though armed soldiers stood to either side, Rozetti pounded on the door and shouted: "Mangus the Magician is here."

We waited. Mangus's breathing was labored. He was, I realized, frightened. *Do something*, I told myself.

I took one of Mistress Sophia's coins from my tunic pocket and held it before Rozetti. Then I rubbed my hands together and, moving quickly, made it appear as if the coin had disappeared. It was the same trick I'd done for Mistress.

The tax collector was startled.

So was my master.

I didn't stop. I reached out and made it seem as if I pulled the coin out of Rozetti's nose, which caused him to blink with fright. When I laughed, his face turned crimson red with embarrassment. Worse, he yanked his dagger from his belt.

I jumped back.

The next moment, "Enter!" was called from the other side of the door and it swung open.

Signor Rozetti, face full of rage, was obliged to step aside.

There, I told myself, *that showed him*. But when Mangus and I walked into the room, the tax collector followed. *Not good*, I thought.

At the far end of the room, King Claudio sat on his gold-encrusted throne, which was placed upon a raised platform. Rozetti stood by the king's side. Face full of wrath, he glared at me.

Maybe I shouldn't have done that trick, I admitted to myself, and tried to put my mind to King Claudio.

The king was a short, heavy-faced man of middling years, with a squared beard surrounding a frowning mouth. Bulky gold chains drooped from around his neck. His thick-fingered hands, barnacled with jeweled rings, were clasped together. His dark eyes were fixed on Mangus.

Nervous, hat in hand, Mangus stood in place, clearly fearful as to what might happen.

I stayed nearby.

"Closer," said the king.

The old man complied, bowed, and in a cautious voice, said, "My lord, you have asked me to come before you."

"Mangus," proclaimed the king, "I am about to send you into another world."

I was certain my master was about to be put to death.

CHAPTER 3

My master must have had the same thought because the shock of it caused him to sway on his feet. I reached out to steady him. This time, he did not wave me away.

"My lord," Mangus said in a panicky voice, "what have I done to displease you so that you can think of such a dreadful act? Be assured, I am more than happy to do anything that may help you. But by all that is holy, I swear, I've heeded your order and stopped performing magic. Even then, every bit of magic I ever did was pretend, mere sleight of hand. Entertainment for the gullible. A way to earn my bread. These days, I do nothing but remain at home with my loving wife, Sophia, and devoted servant, Fabrizio, living the private, thoughtful life of an old philosopher."

"Have no worries, Mangus," bellowed the king. "You've done nothing to affront me — this time. It's because you are a philosopher, the only one in Pergamontio, that I require your help."

Mangus bowed. "My lord," he said, sounding relieved, "to share my reasoning is to share my heart. I am happy to do anything to help you."

"Mangus," said the king, "may I present our royal tax collector, Lorenzo Rozetti. Signor Rozetti, tell Mangus the Magician what you told me last night."

Rozetti bowed and extended his right hand in a gesture of fake courtesy. When he did, I noticed a pinkie was missing. The gesture made sure I saw that he had fought with that dagger of his.

"Your Majesty," said Rozetti in his shrill voice, "last night I informed you that the royal treasury is low. My lord, you are fast running out of money."

"And how do I raise money?" asked the king.

"Taxes, my lord," said the royal tax collector. "At the moment, you take sixty percent of all profits earned in your kingdom."

"Then why am I lacking in funds?"

"Because, my lord, your ungrateful subjects are dishonest about the money they make."

"Explain."

"They hide their profits, my lord. That's to say, despite your constant kindness, they lie and cheat."

"Go on."

"If you were able to discover the true profits your subjects made, you could take more taxes, say *seventy-five* percent."

"Excellent idea. Mangus," the king continued, "have you any response to what Signor Rozetti just said?"

"Forgive me, my lord," said the old man, his voice full of puzzlement. "I know nothing about taxes. I earn no money and live only on the pension you have bestowed."

"In other words," said the king, "without me, you would starve."

"True, my lord. Then . . . what has your problem with taxes have to do with me?"

"Does the name," said the king, "*Luca Pacioli* mean anything to you?"

Mangus grew thoughtful. "Luca Pacioli is an Italian Franciscan, a friar, and one of the better philosophers of our age."

"Do you know his writings?" asked the king.

"My lord, if I'm not mistaken, I have one of Friar Luca's works in my library. But I think he writes about mathematics, so I've not studied him closely. Having so little money, I just count on my wits."

The king, unamused, frowned. "Is not mathematics part of philosophy?" he demanded.

"It is, my lord."

"Do you," the royal tax collector asked Mangus, "know anything about the city called . . . Venice?"

"Venice?" replied a perplexed Mangus. "I've heard it said it is marvelously wealthy. Beyond that, I know little."

The king leaned forward. "Mangus, people say this Venice is a city like no other. 'Another world.' 'A city of magic.' 'The richest place on earth.' At least, its government is. Tell us why, Signor Rozetti."

"Because," replied the royal tax collector, "the traders of Venice are required to use a secret method of bookkeeping — an accounting system — that reveals their actual profits. Which means the government can take more in taxes. The method works like magic. It makes money from the air. That's why the city is so wealthy."

Except the poor people, I thought.

"But, my lord," began Mangus, "I don't —"

The king cut him off. "Listen to me, Mangus. This philosopher mathematician, this Luca Pacioli, lives in Venice, where he is well-known. Rozetti has a friend in the government there who has informed him that Pacioli has written a book that explains how to use this magic accounting method. Moreover, it appears the friar is about to print that book — in Venice — with that terrible new German machine, the printing press. There will be many copies. That means *many* will learn this bookkeeping method. That in turn means people will find countless ways to get around it.

"But if *I* alone knew that method, I'd make a law that required every business in Pergamontio to turn over their accounts to me. I would use that new bookkeeping method to gain real knowledge of people's profits even before they knew what they were. That would allow *me* to take more in taxes. Pergamontio would become as rich as Venice."

"My lord," said Mangus, "I still don't understand. What does this have to do with me?"

"Mangus, I hereby order you to go to Venice, this other world, and steal that book with its secret accounting method so it cannot be printed."

"My lord?" said an astonished Mangus. "Steal a book? But why?"

"I just told you: so I can keep the bookkeeping method to myself and make use of it.

"Mangus," continued the king, "didn't you just admit that mathematics is a part of philosophy? Rozetti is a fighter, not a philosopher. You, like Luca Pacioli, are a philosopher, Pergamontio's only one. Therefore, it is you who must go to Venice and acquire that friar's book. I don't care how you get hold of the manuscript. You even have my permission to use your magic to get it. When you bring that manuscript to me, I shall reward you with a great sum, enough to live well for the rest of your life."

I looked at the royal tax collector. There was nothing but anger on his face.

The king went on. "Understand, Mangus, if you fail to bring that book with its accounting method back to me, you will forfeit your life."

There it was. A clear threat to my master's existence.

"But, my lord," Mangus protested. "It's not my nature to be a spy or a thief. Besides, I'm old. Weak. Who knows how long I shall live? I'll never be able to do what you ask. I don't even know where this Venice is."

"You said," returned the king, "'I am more than happy to do anything that may help you.' Very well, then. By my authority, Mangus, you are to bring that manuscript to me. Am I making myself clear?"

Mangus was speechless.

The king reached down by his feet and pulled up a leather bag. "Here is enough money for your travels. Leave at once. Bring that bookkeeping method back. I need cash. Come, Fabrizio, take it."

Impressed that he remembered my name, I went forward and took the bag into my hands. Though small, it was heavy.

"Go," said the king when Mangus did not move. "And remember what will happen if you do not return with Luca Pacioli's book."

A shocked Mangus took three steps back, bowing to

the king each time. Then he bowed to Rozetti, who continued to scowl.

Mangus slowly made his way out of the throne room. I stayed with him, one hand on his arm to keep him steady. My other hand clutched the king's money. As we went along, I realized that the royal tax collector was just behind us. Though my back was toward him, I could sense his anger. But as we made our way through the Castello, all I was thinking about was this city of Venice, this other world.

Mathematics? I knew nothing beyond Roman numbers. I lived on Master and Mistress's charity and only used coins to run household errands or for magic tricks. Luca Pacioli? I cared nothing for this friar or his book. Or his accounting method.

What thrilled me was that King Claudio had given Mangus permission to go to that magic city and use magic. I hoped my master heard. You may be sure I had. In fact, I don't think I was ever so excited in my whole life. I absolutely had to get Mangus to travel to this magical Venice. Because once I was there, I could finally become a true magician.

CHAPTER 4

CAUGHT UP IN OUR OWN THOUGHTS, MANGUS AND I didn't speak as we made our way out of the Castello. But as I was guiding my faltering master into the carriage, the royal tax collector sidled up to me, squeezed my neck, and said into my ear: "Be advised, boy, don't think I am finished with your master or you. Make no mistake: I intend to get that book along with the king's reward."

Once inside the cab, Mangus sat slumped, head bowed, hands folded together, an image of despair. Clutching the king's money bag, I sat across from him.

"Please, Master," I said, trying to hide my enthusiasm. "This place you are required to go, this . . . Venice . . . can you tell me anything about it?"

Mangus shook his head. "I can do no more than repeat what the king said. It seems to be in another world."

"He said it's magical. Is that true?"

"I know nothing."

"Master, if you don't know anything, how can you go there?"

"Fabrizio, the king has given me no choice. I must learn where Venice is, travel there, find that Franciscan friar, steal his unprinted book with its accounting secret, and bring it to the king. If I do all that, I shall gain wealth. Fail and my life will be over. Refuse to try and I'll lose my pension. That means we shall starve. But if I take such a journey, Fabrizio, I'll no doubt die from the effort. In short, whatever I do brings misfortune."

"But, Master, if, as the king said, this Venice is a magical world, you might gain new sorcery skills, new fortune."

Mangus pointed a crooked finger at me. "Magic, superstitions, secret charms — Fabrizio, it's all gibberish. How many times must I say it? The way to solve problems is with *reason*. Your belief in magic is useless."

"But, Master, the king gave you permission to use it."

"I have no magic to use," he replied.

"Master, you must know *some*."

"Fabrizio," Mangus shouted, "there is no such thing as magic!"

"If you say so, Master," I said in haste, not wishing to

upset him any more than he already was. Except, I didn't believe him. *He must* — I told myself — *know some magic.*

Wasn't he famous because of his magic? Fame doesn't completely lie.

I put my mind to getting him to Venice.

"Master," I said, "I hope you don't think you're too old for such a journey."

"Being old is in itself a journey."

"Please, Master, a journey is never over until there's no further place to go."

"The last place I can go is my grave. I'd rather stay at home."

"Don't fret, Master, I'll travel with you."

"Yes, donkeys do best with an attendant."

"With permission, Master, who is the donkey?"

"You are free to choose."

"Master, a servant does well when his master does well."

"And a servant suffers when his master suffers," Mangus said. "If I go, and you come with me, I will insist on one thing."

"Of course, Master, anything."

"There can be none of your foolish magic. Why did you do the trick upon Signor Rozetti?"

"To show up his arrogance and gain respect."

"Did you?"

"I think so."

Mangus shook his head. "As I've told you countless times, your magic tricks cause trouble. People think it's real magic and grow fearful. Fear makes people feel stupid. When they feel stupid, they become angry. Anger provokes harm. Learn that logic."

I thought of the threat Signor Rozetti whispered into my ear as we got into the carriage. Did it worry me? Let it be admitted, all my thoughts were about this magical city.

"As for going to this . . . Venice," continued Mangus. "Even if I wished to go there, I have no idea where it is."

"With permission, Master, I'll find out."

"You'll have to. I haven't the strength. Now, for once, stop your babble. I must think of some way to avoid the king's order. Hopefully, I have a book by Friar Pacioli in my study. Forgetfulness is God's gift to aged people, so they will stop thinking about how old they are. If I can find that book, I won't have to go."

"Master," I pleaded, "if you just used a bit of your magic, you might —"

"I know no magic!" said Mangus.

I shut my mouth. To cheer him up, I reached into the bag the king had given us and pulled up the largest, brightest coin I could find. It glittered. "The king gave you bright new gold money, Master," I said.

"It's probably fake."

I scratched the coin. Sure enough, the gold came right off.

Mangus waved his hand in disgust and shut his eyes.

I put the coin away.

But as far as I was concerned, Mangus must go to this Venice. Good. I'd never been away from Pergamontio. I'd see the world. A wonderful thing. But again, best of all if I went there, I had no doubt: I'd become a great magician.

CHAPTER 5

When the carriage stopped in front of our house, I helped Mangus out. Mistress Sophia, her eyes looking strained, was waiting at the door. Mangus paused to squeeze her hand but said nothing. Instead, he moved toward his study to search — I had little doubt — for Brother Luca's book.

I was hoping it wouldn't be found.

"Fabrizio," asked Mistress Sophia, "what happened at the Castello? My husband looks sick."

"Master is fine, Mistress. Just tired." I handed her the king's money bag.

"And this?"

"Money from the king so Master can go to another world."

"What are you talking about?"

"The king ordered Master to go to Venice."

"Venice? Where is that? And why go there?"

"It's a fabulously rich city, Mistress. And Master must go there and bring back a book that has a magical way of making money. If Master doesn't fetch that book, the king says there will be no more money for you and he to live."

"Fabrizio, this is folly. My husband is too old to travel."

"The king insists, Mistress. So I need to find out where Venice is as fast as I can. With permission, if you are taking a journey, it helps to know where you are going."

"Thank you, Fabrizio. Let's pray it's close. But understand, if he goes, I'll have to stay behind. I'm not strong enough to travel. And, to be sure, neither is he."

"Have no worries, Mistress, I'll go with him and take care of everything. And when Master returns with that book, the king will give him — and you — riches."

Next moment, I raced down the street to where Signor Loti sat before his olive oil store. He had a glistening bald head, puffy cheeks, and large hands, which he clasped over his knees as if to keep them attached.

"Good morning, Signor Loti," I said with a bow. "I hope you are well."

"Well enough. Thank you, boy," he returned. "The new-pressed oil is fine today. Does the magician's household need a jar?"

"With permission, Signore, it's not oil we need today but information."

"Ah," said the merchant, "information can be as slippery as oil, but doesn't taste as sweet." When he held out an open hand, I gave him one of the coins Mistress Sophia had given me.

"Now then," said Signor Loti, "what would you like to know?"

"King Claudio has ordered my master to go to Venice. But he has no idea where that city is. Do you know anything about it?"

"Venice?" Signor Loti pushed his chin forward and scratched his grizzled neck. "Venice is in Italy."

"With permission, Signore, where is Italy?"

He pointed to the ground. "Right here. Where we live."

"It is? I had no idea. But if this is Italy, where is Venice?"

"Up north, I think."

"Wonderful. If half of Italy — where you say we live — lies to the north and the other half is south, you have just cut our journey in half."

"The one other thing I've heard," continued Signor

Loti, "is that, unlike poor Pergamontio, Venice is the richest place on earth. That's all I know."

"Fantastic," I said. "With Venice so rich, they won't care if my master takes a little something. A million thanks, Signore."

"Glad to be of service," said the oil merchant.

Delighted by what I had learned, I hurried on to the tavern known as the Sign of the Crown. Signor Galda, the owner, was a tall, thin man with a shock of black hair. In the days when Mangus performed his magic shows, he did so at this tavern. Although that had since been prohibited by the king, Signor Galda remained a friend. As I approached, he was taking down the shutters to the old tavern.

"Good morning, boy," he said. "How is the magician today?"

"Signore, King Claudio summoned him to the Castello and ordered him to go to the rich, northern Italian city of Venice. Do you know anything about the place?" I held out a coin, which the tavern keeper managed to take, bite, and put in his pocket, all without looking at it.

"Venice?" mused Signor Galda. "I've been told that the

land of Italy is a peninsula. That's to say, there's a west coast and an east coast. I recollect that Venice lies on the eastern side."

"Grateful thanks, Signore. Since we can now divide the journey east from west, that saves us another quarter of a journey. This means that, moment by moment, even though we have not moved a step, our trip is getting shorter."

"Also," continued Signor Galda, "unlike Pergamontio, which is so empty, Venice is one of the most crowded places on earth. Someone told me a hundred and eighty thousand souls live there."

"One hundred and eighty thousand!" I cried, unable to imagine so many people.

"It seems to be true."

"Excellent," I said. "If Venice has so many people, nobody will notice what we are doing there. Have you any more information?"

Signor Galda shook his head. "Try Signor Cucinello, next door to the church. He's an advocate and will be pleased, for a price, to give you advice about anything and everything even when he knows nothing."

"A trillion true thanks, Signore," I said. "I'll do as you advise."

I hurried along to the Church of Saint Adriano, where a man was sitting behind a small table. It was Signor Cucinello, the advocate, and he was fast asleep.

A small man, Signor Cucinello had a pinched face with a constant scowl, so that his face was as sweet as if he were sucking a lemon. He was always dressed in black: A black robe was draped over his shoulders and a round black cap sat atop his head. On his small table was a pile of parchment and a pot of black ink, into which a black feather pen was sticking.

I set a coin down on his table with a loud *snap*. "Signore," I said, "with permission, may I have the honor of speaking with you?" Signor Cucinello blinked his eyes open.

"As you can see, boy, I'm busy. For that small coin, I can spare only a moment. What do you wish?"

"With permission: King Claudio has ordered my master to travel to northeastern Italy, to the rich, crowded city of Venice. Do you know anything about it?"

"Venice? Its streets are filled with water."

"With permission, Signore, what about horses, donkeys, and carriages?"

"Of no use."

"That's amazing."

"Even more wonderful," continued the advocate, "is how they catch criminals."

"Which is?"

"Lions."

"Real lions?" I asked. I had seen pictures of mighty lions in one of my master's books.

"They are everywhere in Venice. If you wish to accuse someone of a crime, you put the criminal in a lion's mouth. The beast decides if the person is guilty or not by either eating or spitting the person out."

"But, Signore, how do these lions get about in all that water?" I said, delighted by these wonderful facts.

"Venetian lions have wings."

"Wings!" I cried. "Venice must be the most magical place in the world. Anything else?"

Signor Cucinello leaned forward and whispered, "It's also a city full of spies."

"Then two more won't matter," I said, thinking of what we must do when we got there.

"I would advise Mangus not to go," he continued. "It's an old truth: He who travels farthest is most often lost."

"But then, Signore," I returned, "the more lost you are, the more new things you see. Many, many thanks. I will tell my master all you said."

Elated by what I had learned, I decided it would be wise to go into Saint Adriano's church, where I would surely gain more good advice and perhaps a blessing.

Inside the quiet church, near the altar, Father Ambrose was on his knees, in prayer. Older than Mangus, he was full of kindness and thought to be wise.

I dropped a coin in the box marked "For the Poor." The priest looked about. "Ah, Fabrizio, have you something to confess?"

"Father, with permission, I assure you, I have been sinless since I last saw you."

"Dear boy, to think of yourself as free from sin is, I must tell you, a sin."

"Forgive me, Father, but I'm in a hurry. I need to take

a trip, but I promise, out of my profound respect for you, I will sin enough to spend a day confessing when I return."

"See that you do."

I told the priest about the king's order that Mangus go to Venice. "Do you know anything about the city?"

"Nothing good," said the priest with a shake of his head. "First, the people there do not always follow the Holy Roman Church, and as a result, they have no God-anointed king."

"Father, how can people live without a king?"

"They have a republic."

"Forgive my ignorance, Father: What is a republic?"

"A place where the noble people make the mistake of not asking God to provide a king but select their own. Since the people there are not always faithful to the church, God keeps the sun away from them. Venetians live in constant gloom."

"Father," I said, "this Venice must be the most unusual place on earth."

"Be advised, Fabrizio, God prefers the usual. The unusual is the devil's work."

I ducked my head to receive the priest's blessing and then ran for home, eager to tell Mangus all I had learned.

Halfway home, I came upon an old woman sitting on the side of the street, a chipped begging bowl before her. Her face had as many lines as a spider's web, with eyes rimmed in red. Ragged gray hair hung about her shoulders, on which was draped a ragged shawl. I stood before her.

"What do you want with me, boy?" the woman grumbled.

"With permission, mistress, you look like you have traveled far."

"I have," the woman said. "Years of roaming have made me rich in knowledge. Alas, in this world, that kind of richness buys no bread." She picked up her wooden bowl and held it up. I dropped a coin into it.

"Might you," I asked, "with all your travels, be able to tell me the best way to go to the city of Venice?"

"Venice? It's the oddest place on earth."

"Have you been?" I said.

"I'm afraid so."

Ecstatic to meet someone who had been there, I said,

"Afraid? With permission, why should that be?"

"The people who live there hide their faces with masks."

"Masks?"

"They're very shy and don't wish to show their faces. And when they speak, every other word is 'money.'"

"Do you know how to get there?"

"If you are foolish enough to go, travel forty miles east to the city of Bari. In Bari, you'll have reached the sea. From there, go north to Venice, which is a cluster of islands in that sea. Just find a boat that has legs."

"Legs?"

"Such boats can walk across the water."

"Walk across water?" There seemed to be no end to the magic of Venice.

"I promise you, Venice is the strangest place on earth."

"Thank you, mistress."

Wild with delight, I raced home. Now all I had to do was make sure my master got to Venice.

CHAPTER 6

I BURST INTO MANGUS'S STUDY. "MASTER, I'VE learned the most wonderful things about Venice."

"Tell me."

"It may be found in the northeast corner of Italy, which — as I have discovered — is the country we are standing on. To get to Venice, we'll need to travel forty miles east to the city of Bari. Once there, we must find a boat with legs that can walk on water and take us to that fantastical city, which is a bunch of islands.

"Another thing: More people live in Venice than anywhere else in the world, so no one will notice us. Also, the Venetians are so rich, they won't care if we take whatever it is King Claudio wishes to have.

"And, Master," I rushed on, "when we get there, we'll find all the streets are filled with water."

"Fabrizio —"

"Wait, Master, there's more. Venetians are very bashful, so they hide their faces behind masks. Also, they only speak about money, so you can't understand them.

"Another thing, Master: Venetians don't follow the Holy Roman Church and thereby refuse to have an anointed king. In their ignorance, they choose their own ruler. But God punishes them by keeping the city in mist and fog, which is good because we won't be seen.

"Just one more thing, Master. When a Venetian is accused of a crime, that person is stuffed into the mouth of a lion, a lion with wings, and these lions, being the city judges, decide your fate. If you don't know what a lion looks like, I can show you a picture in one of your books.

"Master," I said, exhausted by talking so fast, "Venice is the most magical place in the world. With permission, if you wish my humble advice, from someone who loves you and only wants the best for you, go there immediately."

"Fabrizio," said Mangus, "did you make these things up?"

"Master, everything I said is true." I put a hand to my heart. "The wisest people in Pergamontio told me these things."

He smiled. "Fabrizio, most of what you told me is impossible."

"Forgive me, Master, but things are impossible only when you know nothing about them."

Mangus dismissed the idea with a wave of his hand. "When looking for that Pacioli book, I found a chart that tells me that Venice is indeed in northeastern Italy. That means we shall first have to go to Bari. As for the rest: Flying lions. Boats with legs. Masks. Pure fantasy. I'm sure Venice is quite ordinary. My chief hope is that it's not very hard to reach and that I have enough strength to travel there and back."

"Master," I said, "though I have never left Pergamontio, I have looked out from our city walls. I promise you, using reason — as you are always urging me to do — the world is flat. That means the city of Bari will be easy to reach."

"As for that," said Mangus, "I have one hope."

"What is that?"

Mangus gazed at his bookshelves and sighed. "The truth is, I come to doubt my memory. I think I have a book by this Brother Luca. If it has the accounting secret King Claudio desires, I won't have to travel."

"I'll look hard for it, Master," I said even as I sincerely hoped I'd never find it.

"That would be kind, Fabrizio. While you look, I'll tell my good wife what I've been ordered to do."

As soon as Mangus left his study, I looked over his almost a hundred volumes. I had no doubt Master owned every book in the world.

Though reluctant, I started my search, and after I had pulled out some forty volumes, I opened one and read the words: *Luca Pacioli.*

A bolt of disappointment pierced me. This book had to be written by the same Venetian philosopher that King Claudio talked about. What if it contained the secret bookkeeping method? We would never go to Venice.

I examined the title: *On the Power of Numbers.*

Upset, I flipped through the pages and began to read. To my surprise, it had nothing to do with money. It was a book of puzzles, proverbs, number games, and . . . *magic* tricks. When I saw those, my heart thumped with joy. This friar, this Brother Luca, was a magician.

My desire to go to Venice redoubled, for now, more than anything, I wanted to meet this friar.

I admit, I knew I should have given the book to Mangus, but I was afraid that if he knew Friar Pacioli was a magician, he would not travel to Venice. That would mean that *I* could not go there.

I did what my master always said to do: turn to reason.

If I went to Venice, I would learn all kinds of true magic, which I would use only to help Master and Mistress to thank them for all the kindness they had shown me. To begin, I would restore them to perfect health.

Then, too, the king promised Mangus that when he came back with Pacioli's accounting method, he would give him riches. That would be a wonderful thing — for Master and Mistress.

It was clear then that the best thing for Master to do was to go to Venice. However, since Mangus was old and feeble, I must do him the favor of helping him get there. All of which is to say that since I was such a good servant, it was up to me to take charge of the trip.

Having come to that well-reasoned conclusion, I put Pacioli's *On the Power of Numbers* under my tunic and climbed up to my attic room, where Mistress or Master never went. Once there, I placed the book beneath my straw mattress. Then I returned to the first floor and went about my chores.

Some hours later, Mangus came to me.

"Fabrizio," he asked, "by some good fortune did you find a book by that Friar Pacioli?"

"Master, in all honesty, I can tell you it's not on your shelves. Nor is it on the floor of your study."

"Then," said Mangus, "I have no choice. I must do as the king says. Now, take some of the king's money and buy a donkey. We shall leave tomorrow morning for Venice. But remember, none of your magic tricks or superstitions."

"Never." I put a hand to my heart. "I swear it."

"Good. I'm trusting you, Fabrizio."

"Thank you, thank you, thank you," I said, and gave Mangus a hug and then ran off.

Using the king's money, I bought a donkey, an old beast with gray fur, a white nose, and long ears. I tried to find one that had, as many do, a furry cross on its back. From my study of omens, I knew that if you sit on such a donkey's cross, it brings good luck on your travels. Alas, I was unable to find one and had to get a donkey that didn't have the cross.

That was troubling. Indeed, not finding a donkey with a cross on its back proved an evil omen because, sure enough, that night, something frightening happened.

It was late when I completed the last of my chores, scrubbing kitchen pots, and climbed the ladder to my attic room. Once there, I pulled off my boots, loosened my rope belt, and dropped down on the straw bed, the sole piece of furniture in the room.

As I lay there, aware that the book by Brother Luca was under my back, I kept thinking about all the extraordinary things I had learned about the city of Venice. I was too excited to sleep, and my attic room, with its low roof and close space, felt airless. I got up, went to the front window, and stuck my head out into the cool night sky.

I breathed in the air, which smelled of olive oil, bread, and flowers. The cathedral bells tolled twelve times to signal midnight. *How ordinary*, I thought. *How dull. Magical Venice*, I told myself, *will be much more exciting.*

As I remained there, I heard steps moving along our street. With the evening curfew having rung long ago, no one was supposed to be on the streets.

All the same, someone was coming.

Worse yet, the person stopped in front of our house. Though I leaned far out the window, I was unable to see a face. But I did see someone lift an arm and stretch out a hand, which was illuminated by the lamplight.

My heart sank: The figure was pointing their first and second fingers — a V shape — toward our house. It was *the sign of the evil eye.*

In the whole world, that was the worst of wicked curses. Without a doubt, someone was putting a dreadful spell on my master to make sure that he (and I) did not bring that book to King Claudio. In other words, Mangus and I had not gone one step toward Venice, and we were already in grave danger.

The figure moved on. For a moment, I thought of rushing down to the street, catching up to him, and demanding this person release my master from the curse.

No. Master always told me he didn't trust curses or signs — such as the evil eye. Foolish man. He called them idle superstitions, of which he had no use or fear.

Besides, if my news dissuaded Master from taking the

trip to Venice, King Claudio would punish him. Life would become harsh. Master and Mistress would suffer. And I, who had nothing, would have less than nothing.

Yes. Master *must* go to Venice.

Of course, now I would need to be extra vigilant. Resourceful. Clever. *A lucky thing,* I told myself, *that Master has me for a servant.*

I went back to bed but first made sure my boots were standing upright because I had read that if your boots topple the day before you travel, it means you'll have an unfortunate journey.

Then, to prepare, I practiced some of my magic tricks: making coins appear and disappear. I pulled them from my nose and ears. I swallowed them whole and brought them back. I made them change shape and color.

Then I took up my tarot cards and rolled them in my hands, making them disappear and reappear. One card, two cards, three cards, four cards.

All this practice gave me great confidence. I lay upon my bed and could barely wait for the morning.

CHAPTER 7

THOUGH I WAS READY TO DEPART AT DAWN, MANGUS moved slowly. I had to work hard not to show my exasperation, by cleaning halls and tidying books in his study. A good thing, too: In his room, I found a rusty old nail. Knowing that touching iron brings good luck, I put the nail into my pocket so I'd always be able to reach it.

Meanwhile, Mistress Sophia filled two straw baskets, one with blankets, bread, and drinks, and the other with warm clothing.

Even though she said nothing further on the matter, it was clear she understood Mangus must travel. But when I strapped the baskets to the donkey's back, I still had to wait for my master. Exasperated, I touched that nail in my pocket. It worked. Master got up and ate his breakfast.

After Master Mangus and Mistress Sophia exchanged loving farewells, I helped Mangus get up on the donkey's back, wrapped him in his wool cape, set his cap over his ears, and fitted gloves on his hands. I also secured the king's money in one of the baskets. I gave Mistress Sophia two hugs, plus four cheek kisses, which were returned.

"My dear husband is neither strong nor well," she whispered into my ear. "Take loving care of him."

"With all my heart, Mistress. But who will take care of you?"

"I've arranged for Donna Gianna to come and help me. But, Fabrizio, at moments like these, I wish I had another like you."

"I'll try to bring someone back," I said with a smile.

"Off you go," she said, adding, "God send you ease so you may return with that special book."

With that blessing, I grasped the rope tied around the donkey's neck and started along the road. Though I was eager, there were tears in my master's eyes, which caused me a dip of doubt: *Am I doing the right thing by encouraging this trip?* I reminded myself anew that I was doing it for Master and Mistress. I looked back: She was standing on the street, her face full of sadness. Hopefully, when we returned, I could make both happy again.

From the worn cobblestone streets, we passed through

the ancient gates of the city walls, into another world. I had never been beyond Pergamontio, so I was eager to see everything. To my disappointment, however, all I observed was dry land with a few low hills and now and again some ravines. I did notice some stone farmhouses, sheep, and a few skinny goats. Some olive trees. We passed no other travelers.

As we plodded on, I turned to Mangus. "Master, aren't you excited about going to Venice?"

"I have but two desires, Fabrizio: that I find this book by Brother Luca quickly and that I survive our journey so I can return to my dear wife. As for Venice, I can't be excited about what I can't see."

"Perhaps, Master, I'm excited because I've seen nothing of the world. This," I confessed, "is the first time I've left Pergamontio."

"Be assured, Fabrizio, the best part of seeing the world is that one sees one's soul. The bigger your world, the freer you are. If a tiny part of that nonsense you were told about Venice proves true, you'll discover many marvels within yourself."

"I hope so," I said, and tried to walk faster. But the donkey would have none of it. As a result, it was not until late afternoon that we reached a village of some forty houses.

"Enough for the first day," Mangus announced. "We'll stay the night."

We found the town's sole inn with its brick-laid courtyard and two tables. At one of the tables sat two young men who wore the smocks and sandals of peasants. They were playing with dice, the rattle of their throws the only sound disturbing the silence.

When Mangus and I came into the courtyard, the two men gazed at us intently. One of the men gave the other a nudge. I noticed the prod and took it to mean that these men were not used to seeing strangers.

Within the inn was a hearth with a welcome fire, over which a good-smelling soup hung, attended by a welcoming innkeeper. No one else was there.

I arranged for a room.

"I had best lie down," said Mangus. "So far to go and I'm already tired. Fabrizio," he added with a sigh, "I wonder if I shall survive this."

"Of course you will," I promised. Still, I was troubled that my master was weary after just one day of our journey. It was a reminder of how fragile he was and that I must take good care of him. After making certain Mangus was settled in our room, resting under the blankets we had brought, along with some fresh bread and some good soup, I went down to put the donkey in the stable. Once that was done, I sat at one of the courtyard tables. The two men were still playing with dice. I watched their game.

One of the men glanced at me. Though he said nothing, he gave his companion a poke, as if to say, "He's back."

I thought: *Pokes promise problems.* In fact, as the two men continued to play, their quiet made me so uneasy, I studied them anew.

They were young, with a suggestion of considerable strength. Their faces were tanned and showed no emotion. I decided they were contemplating something ill.

Their troubling silence was broken only by dice rattling on the table. But after a while, one of the men jabbed the other man as if to say, "Get on with it."

The other man turned to me and said, "Are you and the old man pilgrims heading for Jerusalem?"

"No, Signore. We're going to Bari, and then on to Venice."

The two peasants exchanged looks.

"Ah, well," said one of the men, "Bari is a fine city with a fine cathedral. Saint Nicholas, that saint who protects children, is buried there. Since you're so young, you'd be wise to go and pray that he looks after you. But Venice . . ." The man shook his head. "No, I wouldn't go there if I were you."

"With permission, Signore, why not?"

"Venetians are very suspicious of strangers. They show it by having dreadful prisons. Why are you going?"

Having no reason to be secretive, I said, "There is a Franciscan friar there, Brother Luca Pacioli. My master, who is one of the great philosophers in the world, wishes to find a book he wrote."

"Ah." The way the man said it made me uneasy.

"Where are you from?" the other man asked.

"Pergamontio."

The two men exchanged another look. When one of them nodded, they got up and came to where I was sitting and stood to box me in. One of them put a heavy hand on my shoulder.

I felt like a rabbit in a trap.

"You seem like an honest boy," said one of the men. "And your old master appears harmless. But I must tell you that someone gave us money to keep your master here."

The hand on my shoulder was so tight, I was unable to move.

"Holding him here isn't something that matters to us," said the other man. "But to be honest, the money that fellow gave us was considerable."

"What . . . what do you intend to do?" I said, trying to think two things: Who that fellow was and how I could deal with these men.

"On the one hand," added the other, "we're not violent. On the other hand, we can always use money. We might have to keep you and your master here.

"If you gave us some money — we'd be happy to strike a bargain and let you go. It's all the same to us."

I glanced at the table where the dice were still sitting. They gave me an idea.

"I'm sure we can," I said. "But, with permission, Signori, I suggest the amount we give you should be decided by your dice. Whatever numbers I throw can be what we'll give you."

The two men looked at each other. "Why not?" said one to the other. "By Saint Boniface, it's always better to let fate be in charge."

One of the men fetched the dice and handed them to me.

I stood up and shook the dice hard. With quick movements, I made it appear as if the dice vanished.

The men stared at me with wonder. "What did you do with those dice?" one of them demanded.

"They are in your ears," I announced, and plucked one of the dice from one man's ear, the second from the other.

The look on the men's faces turned from bewilderment to fright.

"I warn you," I proclaimed. "My master and I have great magic. As you can see, I'm not afraid to use it."

I shook the dice in my hands again and made it appear as if they vanished altogether. "If you don't leave us alone," I said, "I'll make both of you disappear in the same way."

The two men fled from the courtyard.

Delighted by what I had achieved, I went to the room where Mangus was resting. Feeling obliged to tell him something, I said, "Master, unhappy news."

He looked up.

"Someone is trying to do us harm."

"What makes you say that?"

"Those two men in the courtyard below told me that a man gave them money to keep us here."

"Do these men intend to do that?"

Not wishing to share with Master that I had used magic tricks to frighten the men away, magic, which I had promised I'd not do, I said, "I talked to them, and they became uneasy about doing such a wicked thing. They went away, promising to leave us alone."

"Now, Fabrizio, as you say," said Mangus, "nothing truly bad has happened. I suspect those men were playing a joke on you. Or just wanted money."

"But, Master, as people say, if you wish to see the truth, it's better to open your eyes."

"True," replied Mangus, "but eyes are for seeing, not guessing."

With that, he lay back, shut *his* eyes, and was soon asleep.

I ate some bread and cheese and then lay down against the door to keep anyone from coming in. I slipped into a night of easy sleep, feeling ready and capable of protecting Mangus from any danger.

CHAPTER 8

In the morning, I let Mangus sleep while I crept down to peek into the inn's courtyard to see if those two men had come back. To my relief, they had not. But the woman who ran the inn looked at me with unease and was not as friendly as she had been when we first arrived. She must have heard about my magic.

The notion that she thought me a magician pleased me. It made me feel that, despite what I had promised Mangus, I should use tricks to deal with any trouble we might encounter. They worked and kept us safe. And I could do it without Master knowing.

After Mangus and I had our breakfast of bread, cheese, and milk, we resumed our eastward journey toward the city of Bari. As before, I walked and led the donkey while Mangus traveled on the beast's back. There was almost no talk. I kept thinking about how I had tricked those two men. Master was lucky to have me as his servant.

It was midmorning when we came to the top of a high hill. Down below lay an entire walled city.

"Bari," Mangus announced.

I could see right away that Bari was far bigger than Pergamontio. Even more astonishing was what lay beyond it: an immense, flat gray-blue vastness that stretched as far as I looked. It was unlike anything I'd ever seen before.

"Master," I said, "all that flatness . . . What is it?"

"The sea."

"But . . . it seems to have no . . . end."

"Perhaps not altogether endless, but vast."

"What is it made of?"

"Water."

"All of it?"

"To be sure."

"Can . . . you drink it?"

"I wouldn't."

"But where is Venice?"

"Somewhere. As you were told, we'll need a boat to get there."

"With legs," I reminded him. "How will we find one?"

Mangus smiled. "Ah, Fabrizio, I hope I've taught you:

He who is fearful of appearing unwise by not asking questions *is* unwise."

"But, Master," I said, "what if you ask the wrong question?"

"To be sure, ignorant questions bring ignorant answers."

"But that would mean," I said, "it takes wisdom to become wise."

"A wise answer," said Mangus with a smile.

We moved downhill and approached the gates of Bari. They were surrounded by people jostling to get past armed guards watching to see who entered.

Once we passed through the city gates, we entered upon a muddle of slender stone-paved streets. On both sides were three- and four-floor buildings made of stone or wood, with no space between. On the ground level were open shops and stalls, selling goods. Higher up was where people lived. The air smelled of food, sweat, and dung.

As for noise, my ears were filled with constant chatter, high and low voices, cries, and shouts of "Buy this," "Buy that," more than I had ever heard on Pergamontio's quiet streets. Most people were dressed simply, though here and there I saw folks of obvious wealth. Everyone seemed to know where they were going except us.

"Look for an inn," Mangus called above the din.

As I tried to make sense of the crowded city while searching for a place where we might stay, I kept gazing about. It was as I glanced behind, I saw — or thought I saw — a peacock feather rising above the crowd. It seemed familiar, and it took a moment to realize it was like the feather I had seen on Rozetti's hat. I instantly wondered: Was he the person who had paid those men at the inn to keep us from going on toward Venice?

I looked again but was jostled by the crowd. When I recovered, I no longer saw the feather. I told myself that it must have been a coincidence. What had Mangus told me? "Eyes are for seeing, not guessing." Indeed, though I kept turning about and looking, I saw no further sign of it. As we moved deeper into the old city, I put aside my worry.

Mangus, sitting high on the donkey, called out, "There, Fabrizio. An inn." He pointed to a hanging sign — THE SAFE HARBOR.

I tied the donkey's lead to a pole, then hastened inside the small inn and inquired about a room. A welcoming innkeeper with a head of white hair and big ears said space was available. He asked, "Have you come for the spice fleet?"

"With permission, Signore," I replied, "what's that?"

"The galleys."

"Forgive my ignorance, Signore, what are galleys?"

"The Venetian boats. They're supposed to come in today and stay the night. Tomorrow they'll head north to Venice."

I saw my opportunity. "Signore, that's exactly where my master and I need to go. Do you think I might secure a place on one of those boats and gain passage there?"

"People do so all the time. Ask a ship capitano."

"With permission, where can I find one?"

"On the ships." The innkeeper pointed. "Go downhill through the city. You can't fail to reach the beach and water. Farther along, there's a peninsula where you'll find wharves. If the Venetian fleet arrives — and it's expected any hour — it will tie up there. Capitani will be on board. Seek one out. Mind, it will cost you. My advice? Accept whatever they offer. At this time of year, there's no saying when the next fleet will go north."

"A billion barrels of blessings, Signore."

I told Mangus what the innkeeper had said. "Master, if we're lucky enough to arrange for passage, we'll be able to get to Venice quickly. Have I permission to take money?"

"Of course."

I secured a room and led Mangus up the steps to the second floor and settled him in to take his rest. I brought up our baskets of provisions, took care of the donkey, picked out some coins, and then went off in search of a ship capitano, hurrying downhill through Bari's teeming, twisted streets.

As I moved along, I tried to take notice of things such as a FOR SALE sign, a stout lady standing before a table of vegetables she was selling, a huge silver fish hanging by its tail outside a fish store, anything that might enable me to find my way back to the inn and Mangus.

I also kept my eyes open to see if I was being followed,

but the city was so crowded I could not be sure. I did notice other men with feathers in their hats. Realizing that feathers seemed to be the fashion, I put the tax collector firmly out of mind. Besides, Bari was full of interesting things — here, a bead shop; there, a tiny curio store; another, a place that sold bright swords, all thoroughly fascinating.

I continued downhill until the city ended and what lay before me was nothing but the open sea. No buildings, no people, just a world that had exploded into vast magnitude.

Unable to go farther — unless I stepped into the water, which I was not about to do — I stood on a shelf of sand where low waves rippled in with soft splashes. I looked out. *Where*, I wondered, *is Venice?* To my disappointment, the city was still nowhere in sight.

Not far from where I stood were a few small boats with high prows, bobbing about on the water. Seeing that the men in them had nets and lines in hand, I decided they were fishermen. A few of these small boats were pulled up on the sand.

To my left, just as the innkeeper had told me, was a

peninsula that jutted a good distance into the sea. Many boats clustered around it. I had, of course, seen boats on the small river that went through Pergamontio, but these were larger than I had ever seen before. Some had tall masts. One or two of the bigger boats had furled sails. On and about these ships, men were working.

As I stood there, marveling at the new things I was seeing, I noticed that far out on the sea was what appeared to be a cluster of black bugs. As I watched, puzzled, I realized that they were moving toward the city, which is to say, toward me.

No sooner did I see them than church bells began to ring throughout Bari. Trumpets blared. Drums beat. It was clearly a celebration, but of what I had no idea.

As I continued to stand there, wondering why there was such enthusiasm, people began to gather at the beach. I soon realized that they were looking at those bug-like things while talking excitedly among themselves. I understood; the bells and trumpeting were welcoming whatever was moving toward the city.

Remembering Mangus's advice about asking questions,

I turned to a boy who was standing near me. "What are those things?" I pointed out to the sea.

"The Venetian galley boats," the boy answered. "The spice fleet."

Elated, I turned to look again. As the spots drew closer, I realized I was seeing twenty or so long, low boats, with high prows. All had a single tall pole in the middle, from which hung a sail. Most astonishing of all, I saw that these boats had . . . legs.

Boats with legs!

These legs stuck out from both sides of the boats so that they looked like centipedes walking on the surface of the water. And they were coming forward at high speed.

My immediate thought was *Then everything I was told about Venice is true.* I was overjoyed, sure that my master and I would be able to get to Venice in the magical way I'd been instructed to go.

All the while, city church bells rang, and trumpets blared, while the crowd of onlookers by the sea edge kept growing. Some people were even cheering.

As the boats drew nearer, I realized that they did not have legs. But I had no idea what I was seeing.

"What are those things sticking out from those boats?" I asked the boy who was still close to me.

The boy looked at me as if I were foolish. "What do you think? They're galleys. With oars."

Oars.

I studied the boats. I saw it then: Yes, I now realized, they were oars. They were quite long, and each galley had them on both sides. They moved in perfect unison, sweeping over the water surface, dipping, pulling back, then rising and moving forward again, bringing the boats on, while causing a curl of white foam to rise before each prow.

As the fleet headed for the peninsular wharves, the townspeople — including me — rushed off to meet them. I knew what I must do: arrange for immediate passage. If our innkeeper spoke true, this was our best and perhaps only chance to get to Venice.

CHAPTER 9

BY THE TIME I REACHED THE PENINSULA, THE GALLEYS had tied up at the docks. Once there, I was able to see how big the ships were: long and slender, high-prowed, crowded with crew, decks packed with barrels, bales, and boxes.

Amid the welcoming crowd, I watched as the galley rowers, perhaps as many as 150 from each boat, poured onto the wharves. Their faces were weathered and unshaven, heads tied around with colored cloths. Loose smocks showed off burly sunburned arms. On their feet, low-cut boots. Overall, they seemed a rough, wind-creased, and strong lot. Most of them headed toward the city.

As I wandered along the wharves, I saw many of the rowers kneel and open small sacks upon the wharf planking. Like a busy market day, they were offering things for sale to the gathering crowd. Small bags of spices, ginger, cinnamon, cloves, pepper, and nutmeg called out by name were for sale, plus a variety of objects, such as glass bottles, small knives, and jewelry. I watched, fascinated, as Bari people, with spirited bargaining, bought up what was offered.

As I roamed about, I saw a small knife being offered, its handle inlaid with bits of blue. To be sure, they were not jewels but handsome glass. Presented by a young oarsman, the knife lay on a red cloth. As soon as I saw it, I was filled with the desire to have it but told myself I mustn't. I walked past, then stopped, still thinking about that beautiful knife. I had never owned anything so fine. Then I remembered: I had some money.

I walked back.

"What's the cost?" I said, and pointed to the knife.

"Two lira," returned the sailor.

"What is lira?"

The man looked at me with suspicious eyes, as if he couldn't believe I didn't know. "It's what Venetian money is called."

I reached into my pocket and held out some of my Pergamontio coins. The oarsman bent over to look at them, took up a few, and then, to my pleasure, handed me the knife.

I held it in my hands, touched it all over, studied the color bits on its hilt, and fingered its sharp blade.

Pleased with myself, I stowed the knife deep down in my tunic pocket so as not to lose it. Then I wandered on, enjoying the sights of the fleet, the crowd, and all the market bustle.

As I went along, I noticed that on one of the galleys, atop a platform at the stern, a man was standing who seemed different from the ordinary sailors. He wore a wool jacket, leather boots, and a cloth cap on his head. He had placed himself next to the rudder bar and was looking on with an air of authority while observing the hectic scene. As I watched, he now and again called out orders to his crew.

Deciding he must be the galley's capitano, I drew nearer.

"Signor Capitano," I shouted. "With permission, may I have a word?"

The man turned toward me.

"Signor Capitano," I called again, louder. "My master wishes to travel to Venice. Would you have room for the two of us?"

"It will cost you ten lira," returned the man in a shout. "I'll take you if you are here with the money at dawn tomorrow. The voyage north will take two days, and you'll sleep in the hold. Not a lot of comfort," he called back. "But that's the best I can do."

"A barrel of thanks, Signor Capitano," I yelled back. "I promise we'll be here."

I now regretted buying that small knife, which lay in my pocket. I could only hope we had money enough for the journey.

"At dawn," the galley master repeated in a shout. "I won't wait one minute for you."

"We'll be here, Signore," I returned, and spun about, once more very pleased with myself, and eager to tell Mangus what I had arranged.

It was as I turned that I saw — behind me — what looked like a peacock feather, just like the one Rozetti wore. *Was it him?*

Even as I saw the feather, the man wearing it was moving away, becoming lost in the crowd. Next moment, I realized he'd been close enough to hear what I had arranged even to the exact galley and time when we would leave Bari for Venice.

Needing to find out if it was Rozetti, I plunged among the swarms of people. Alas, they were much bigger and taller than me. Though I pushed and shoved, the crowd was too thick, too strong. When I managed to break through, I had lost sight of the feather.

Reminding myself that, beyond all else, I had to protect Mangus, I raced down the peninsula until I was again in the middle of Bari's streets. Once there, I struggled to make my way through the packs of people, all the while searching for our enemy. It didn't matter what direction I turned; I saw no sign of the feather. Fearful I was being watched, I hurried on.

Winded, I halted and gazed about, trying to determine where I was, turning this way and that, searching for something to tell me where I might be. As I stood there, I nervously fingered the knife in my pocket, even as I worked hard to keep from becoming panicky.

Since I had come downhill toward the sea, I ran uphill. First I went to the right, changed my mind, and then went

to the left. As I ran, I often paused and tried to see if I was being followed or some hint that our inn was close. Whenever I stopped, people surged around me. I became even more confused.

All of sudden, everything went black. Something — a bag, a blanket — I had no idea what — had been thrown over my head.

I fought to free myself, but the person who held me proved too strong. As for my furious shouts of protest, they were muffled by what was covering me. Then I felt something — was it a rope? — binding me.

The following instant I was picked up, arms pinned to my sides, and carried off. Not a word was said by my captor.

I wasn't taken far. Within moments, I was flung upon hard ground. What I then heard was something that sounded like the slamming of a door. Unable to move or see, I assumed I had been made a prisoner.

I attempted to free myself, but when I tried to move, I discovered that the covering wrapped around me pinned my arms to my sides. But though my arms were bound,

I managed to move my hands the tiniest bit. Twisting, straining at the binding, I was able to reach a hand into my pocket and grasp the knife I had purchased. I slid it back and forth until I had sliced through my tunic pocket. Then I maneuvered the knife to slash at the bag that covered me. Gaining more movement, I was able to saw through the rope, for that, I discovered, was what held me. Once the rope was severed, I was able to yank away the bag from my head.

I was free.

Except I was not.

A waist-high window with rusty iron bars provided some light, but that only enabled me to see that it was a small storeroom that might as well have been a prison. The room had wooden walls, a dirt floor, nothing else. There was a door, but when I tried to open it, I found it locked.

I feared that someone had captured me to isolate Mangus. If so, my master was in grave danger.

The door, fastened on the outside, would not budge. I used my knife to poke at the rusty iron hinges. To my

disgust, the blade broke in half. It had served me well, but not for long.

I went to the window, through which I saw an adjacent street, no more than an alley. I was able to reach out, but that offered no benefit. I pulled on the old bars. They wouldn't give.

Standing at the window, I saw a few people go by. Whenever they did, I called out "Signore" or "Signora." Alas, the people ignored my calls.

A girl came skipping by. She was wearing an old skirt and a blouse, with a chest pocket. It was the pocket that gave me an idea.

"You there!" I called out, my face pressed against the window bars. The girl stopped, looked about, not sure from where the call had come.

"Over here," I said. Reaching out through the bars, I waggled my fingers. "With permission, I need help."

The girl looked at me with suspicion. "What's the matter?"

"I've been locked in here by mistake. Please, will you open the door?"

The girl started to walk away.

"Listen," I said. "You are going to lose that money in your pocket."

She stopped and looked at me again, her face showing puzzlement. She put her hand to her blouse pocket and patted it. "I have no money," she said.

"Yes, you do. Right in that pocket."

She felt it again. "I do not."

"Come closer and I'll show you."

The girl came up to the window. I stretched out — I had palmed one of my remaining coins in my hand so she was unable to see it — reached into her pocket and pulled out the coin, then offered it to her.

Baffled, the girl took the coin and examined it. "How did you do that?" she asked.

"I'm a magician," I said. "If you open the door to this room, I'll make more money appear in your pocket."

"If you are a magician, why can't you open the door yourself?"

"My magic only works with money."

Looking from the coin to me, the girl studied me,

trying to decide — I thought — if I was telling the truth. Then she moved away, but whether she was going to the door or not, I wasn't sure.

To my great relief, I heard a latch slide open. The door swung out. The girl stood in the doorway. "Make some more money," she said, holding out her hand.

I did the trick again and gave her a coin. As the girl studied it, I bolted past her and began to race uphill. Once again, my magic tricks had served me well. But now I had to get to Mangus.

CHAPTER 10

I WENT ALONG FOR NO MORE THAN A FEW MOMENTS when I recognized our innkeeper — white hair and big ears — walking ahead of me. He looked neither to the right nor left but moved straight on, which made me certain he would lead me to my master. Sure enough, he went right to the Safe Harbor and stepped inside. I waited a few seconds, then went after him into the inn.

No sooner did I enter than the innkeeper greeted me with the words "Ah, there you are. I am pleased to see you well and walking about."

"With permission, Signore, why would I not?'

"I was out on an errand, but my wife was here. A man came by and told her that you had an accident and would not be able to attend your master for a few days."

"Please, Signore, as you can see for yourself, I am fine. May I ask, who brought the message?"

"I have no idea. He spoke to my wife."

"With permission, may I talk to her?"

"She just left to visit with her mother."

"Did she speak to my master before she left?"

"She was in a hurry, so she told me to pass the unhappy message on. I'm glad I don't have to."

"Many thanks, Signore."

I hurried up the steps but stopped halfway. Sitting on a riser, I thought about the message. It must have been from the person who put me in that room. To be sure, locking me up and delivering that message was an attempt to keep us from going on to Venice. Whom had I told we were going to Venice? Those people at the little inn where we stayed. And the innkeeper here. Or, more likely, our enemy watched us come into Bari and then followed us to learn where we were staying. Then they trailed me to the shore and peninsula. They were close when I made my arrangements with that galley capitano. They had heard me.

Next, they captured me and threw me into the room. Knowing where we were lodged, thinking I was trapped, they delivered that false message.

Since I knew the message was untrue, I was sure we still had passage to Venice. All I needed to do was get us to that galley by dawn and, of course, stay close to Mangus.

I rushed up to the room where Mangus was resting.

"Master," I announced, "I have arranged everything. We leave for Venice on a galley at dawn. I must pay our landlord so we can leave on time. That means I must change our money into Venetian money."

Mangus, who didn't seem that interested, only said, "Take what you need."

I returned to the innkeeper. "With permission, Signore," I told him. "We depart on a Venetian galley at dawn. But since we have to leave so early, may I pay you for our room now and take our donkey from your stable and tie him to the post before the door?"

"Of course."

"I have coins from Pergamontio. I'm not sure what they are worth. Will they buy me what are called lira?"

From a box, he gathered one up and held it out. "Here is a lira."

I studied the coin: It had an image of a winged lion.

In turn, the innkeeper examined the Pergamontio money. "I don't know the value of your money," said the man. "I suppose it's worth something." He took what I had, and in exchange, he gave me lira. "That should do." Then he asked, "What takes you to Venice?"

"My master needs to see someone there."

Something in my voice made the innkeeper lean forward. "Is it a secret mission?"

I shrugged with pretend indifference. "My master wishes to visit a man who has written a book."

"Boy, let me give you some advice," continued the innkeeper. "Venice is the mightiest state in all of Italy. The biggest navy in the world. People call the Venetians 'crafty and malignant foxes.' That's because they fear spies the way other people fear bad weather. Always. That galley you will travel on is owned by the government. The merchants rent them. That means that on every one of her galleys, there's a man who works for the government. They call these men Black Robes. They spy on the rest. When they catch someone illegal, the city rewards them.

"The informer might be noble. Or a galley rower. In other words, when you are on that galley, be careful. You may be sure, there will be a Black Robe on the ship."

"Signore, I assure you, we have nothing to hide."

I thanked him and returned to Mangus. The old man was as I had left him, on the bed, reading by candlelight.

"With permission, Master. I have arranged for everything. We leave tomorrow at dawn."

"Excellent, Fabrizio. Wake me when it's time."

I had one last thing to do: I tied up our donkey by the inn's front door.

Back in our room, I blew out the candle and set myself on the floor near the door, determined to stay awake until dawn to get to the galley on time.

I had avoided being held by those two men at the inn. I had guided Master to Bari. I had arranged travel to Venice. Though I had been caught and thrown into a prison-like room, I had escaped with a magic trick and then foiled a plan to keep us from going to Venice. So far, I had dodged the curse of the evil eye. Let it be admitted, I was feeling very good about myself.

Sitting in the dark, listening to the sound of Mangus's breathy sleep, I struggled to keep my eyes open, even as I looked forward to the next day. *Keep awake*, I told myself, but it wasn't long before I fell asleep.

CHAPTER 11

It seemed as if just seconds had gone by when I heard the clanging of church bells and the wail of trumpets. It took me a moment to grasp what was happening: It was dawn, and the city of Bari was saluting the Venetian fleet as it was departing.

I leaped up. "Master, the boats for Venice are going. You must get up."

Mangus opened his eyes and sighed, "Is it morning, Fabrizio?"

"It is, Master, and forgive me, I overslept. Which means you must get out of bed right away. The galleys are leaving for Venice." I pulled at his blanket. He pulled it back. "We have to hurry," I insisted as Mangus and I engaged in a tugging match.

"I'm cold," he said.

"Master," I said, "if you don't get up, we'll miss the galley. If we miss the galley, we may never get to Venice. It will be a disaster."

With much reluctance, Mangus swung his skinny legs

out from under the blanket and gingerly set his bare feet on the cold floor. With something like a groan, while reaching out for my hand, he stood up.

I helped him dress, him sighing and grumbling all the while. Then I needed to find his boots, which, somehow, were lost under the bed. I had to search for his cap, set it on his head, and snatch up our money bag. Though I was feeling frenzied, Mangus refused to move with any urgency. It didn't help that I was angry and embarrassed with myself for falling asleep. All the while, the city church bells were clanging, and trumpets were blaring. It sounded as if they were laughing at me.

When Mangus was ready, I led him out of the room and down the steps of the inn. In the poor light, we needed to go step-by-step like a baby, two feet on each riser, the old man muttering and complaining all the way.

The dawn was cold, the light ashen, but I had done one thing right: Our donkey was there. I struggled to get Mangus on the beast. Then we left the inn, and with me walking, and yanking on the donkey's rope, we headed downhill toward the sea,

Though I struggled to hurry, the donkey showed no inclination to move any faster than he had on previous days. Instead, he plodded forward with deliberate, slow steps. I implored him, pulled at him, but the donkey would not go faster.

To make matters worse, after we had gone some distance, I realized that in haste, I had forgotten our baskets of provisions, clothing, and Master's reading book. My heart sank. There was no time to go back, but thankfully, Master hadn't seemed to notice. Still, I clutched our money bag tighter. Happily, the morning crowds were far less dense than before so at least I didn't have to force my way through. And the low eastern light was increasing, showing the way.

We reached the shore. As soon as we did, I looked toward the peninsula. My heart lurched. Most of the Venetian galleys, oars moving, sails hoisted, were already moving away from the shore, stretched out in a line like ducklings following a mother duck. I stood there, devastated. As if to mock me, the city bells and trumpets continued to clang and bleat. Despite the hour, many townspeople were gathered on the beach, watching and saluting the departing fleet with cheers and shouts. We were too late. I was close to tears.

Then I noticed that on the sandy strip at the edge of the sea was one of those small boats, and a man — he looked like a fisherman — preparing for the day.

I rushed over to him.

"Signore, with a billion baskets of begs, my master must board one of those Venetian ships. Can you take us?"

The fisherman looked at me, at the departing galleys, then back to me. "They are already moving," he said with a shake of his head.

"Signore," I pleaded, "my master must join them."

The fisherman flipped his hand. "It will cost you, and you still might not catch them."

Not knowing what else to do, I blurted out, "I'll give you our donkey."

The fisherman appraised the beast in silence. "I can try," he said. "But I can't promise to get you there."

"Ten trillion thanks, Signore." I dashed back over the sand and pulled Mangus off the donkey.

"That man will take us to the galley," I said.

"Fabrizio, I think —"

"Master!" I shouted, something I had never done before. "You must do as I say."

Then I all but dragged him across the beach to the fisherman's boat. Once there, I managed to get him aboard the boat and seated in the bow.

Mangus turned upon me with anger and confusion. "Is this man taking us out to sea?" he asked.

"To the galleys, Master. To Venice. To Brother Luca's book."

He groaned. "If we must."

"Boy," the fisherman called to me. "Lend a hand."

The fisherman and I pushed the boat — with Mangus in it — across the beach and into the frigid water. Once it was afloat, I scrambled aboard, and the fisherman got in, too.

Standing at the stern, he began to row with one long oar. All I could do was sit, wish there were another oar, and watch anxiously as the fleet of Venetian galleys continued to move farther out to sea.

Working hard, the fisherman guided his boat into deeper waters. That brought on a new sensation; the boat pitched and swayed, making me queasy. What if the boat flipped over? I was unable to swim. No doubt Master couldn't, either. The old man must have had the same thought because he was very pale and gripped his seat with two hands.

I kept my eyes on the galleys, fixing my hopes on the last one in line. It was still next to the wharves, oars not extended, sail not hoisted.

"Go up front," the fisherman called to me as we drew nearer. "Hail the galley that hasn't moved."

I stumbled forward and stood — or at least tried to — and shouted: "Signori, please. With permission. We must board!"

I was beginning to think we would reach her, when I saw the boat fling out oars and hoist her gray sail.

"We need to go faster," I called.

As the fisherman worked his oar harder, that last galley edged away from the wharf.

"Wait," I screamed. "Wait!" I waved my arms like a windmill in a storm.

As we drew closer, I saw that someone on the galley's stern was looking toward us. "We need to board," I yelled.

"We need to board." Then I realized what I had to do.

I shoved my hand into our money bag, felt for the largest coin, and, hoping the metal would gleam in the low morning light, held it up.

It seemed to work. The galley oars — in unison — lifted from the water. The single sail seemed to slacken. The galley was only drifting.

The fisherman's boat drew alongside the galley. Several men on the ship were looking down at us.

"Signori, a gazillion gobs of grace," I wailed. "We need passage to Venice." I kept holding the coin in the air.

The man on the stern — the capitano, I assumed — studied me — or the coin — as if to make an appraisal and then said, "Thirty lira."

I realized that was three times what I had been told before. But this was not the same man. Nor was I sure what money we had left. It didn't matter. There was no choice.

"Agreed!" I cried.

The fisherman maneuvered his little boat up against the galley. Some of the crew came to the side and reached down. I managed to get Mangus onto his feet. The boat's bow dipped. Master wobbled. I steadied him, praying we would not capsize. The galley men leaned over, took hold of Mangus's arms, and hauled him up like a sack of wheat. As they did, his cap fell off, so that his sparse gray hair fluttered in the air like a ragged flag.

"Signori," I screamed. "Don't forget me."

Next moment, I, too, was snatched out of the fisherman's boat, up into the air and onto the galley.

"A billion, trillion thanks," I called to the fisherman as he rowed away.

As for the galley, her oars dropped down to the water with a loud splash and began to move in unison. As the boat jerked forward, I drew a deep, deep breath. I'd done it. We were moving away from Bari toward the magical city of Venice.

CHAPTER 12

WHILE A ROSY-TINTED DAWN SPREAD OVER THE entire eastern horizon, the city of Bari seemed to slide toward the south. North and west offered nothing but gray-blue sea. As the galley cut through the water, there was a constant *swish* along with the *fluff* and *snap* of the single sail, along with the *crash-splash* of 140 oars and water spraying down on the deck like a cold rain.

Mangus and I had been put on the high rudder platform. When I glanced down from where we were, I saw rowers sitting on a lower deck, three men on each slanted bench, seventy oars on both sides of the galley. Every trio worked one long oar. Each oar — as I would learn — weighed 150 pounds.

On the top deck stood a man beating a drum. The rowers moved in unison — forward and back — forward and back — to his beat. Two other officers paced along the galley's upper deck, issuing orders, or rebukes. Four men seemed to oversee the central sail.

Despite the cold air and sea spray, the rowers were

garbed in short tunics and cloth boots. Their arms and knees were bare and deeply sunburned; their faces showed no emotion. They just rowed. But with the repeated pull of all those oars, along with the dip and yaw of the ship, it felt as if we were always leaping forward, making it so hard for me to stand I had to hold on to a rail. As for Mangus, he sat on the deck planking, thin legs stretched before him, back propped up against a barrel. Breathing with effort, he kept rubbing a hand over his face and beard, trying to wipe away sea spray and, no doubt, his confusion.

Two men stood by the rudder bar. One, I decided, must be the capitano, but he was not the one with whom I had bargained the day before. What's more, he was looking right at me, his hand open and extended in a gesture that said, "Give me money."

Having no choice, I made my way to him, holding my money bag, finding it hard to gain footing on the shifting ship. When I reached him, I took out some of my Venetian money and offered it. The capitano scrutinized it. He frowned.

"Is that your money bag?"

"Yes, Signore."

"Give it here," he said, wiggling his fingers, leaving me in no doubt that I must hand over my entire money bag. When I did, he poured out the rest of our money into the palm of his large hand.

"Not even close," he announced, dumping the coins into his own pocket. He tossed the empty money bag back to me.

"With permission, Signore," I said. "That's everything we have."

"You're welcome to get off my ship."

Not knowing what to say or do, I just stood there.

Another man was standing close to the capitano. He was a short fellow, bulked with muscle. His face had unsmiling lips and severe eyes. I wondered who he was and why he was standing next to the capitano, studying me with such intensity.

"Why are you going to Venice?" this man demanded.

Not wishing to say anything about the real reason for our coming, I just said, "My master is looking for books, Signore."

The capitano turned to this man. "Signor Cardano, take them below," he ordered.

"Move on," this Cardano said to me.

With me holding on to my master's arm to keep him from stumbling, we were led down into a dismal hold. Since it was lower than the rowers' benches, we could see their feet. At the ship's bottom was a thick layer of sand in which barrels, bales, and sacks had been placed. The stench of bilge was strong, though there were some sharp smells, which I was unable to identify.

"Remain here," said Signor Cardano as though he had some authority. As he left us, I wondered what position he held on the ship and why he had acted with such rudeness.

All that Mangus and I were able to do was sit in that miserable place. Once, twice, I checked our money bag, trying not to see that it was empty.

"The capitano took all our money," I announced. "He gave me no choice."

"Ah, Fabrizio, even misery costs money."

"As people say, Master, the wages of despair is misery."

I took another deep breath. "At least we are going to Venice."

"I'd rather we were going home."

"Venice is rich and full of magic," I reminded him.

"Fabrizio, taking pleasure from a place before you get there is like drinking from an empty glass of water."

As the galley creaked and groaned, we sat without talking. All I could hear was the endless splash of the oars in rhythm with the beat of the drum.

Mangus said, "How long will this take?"

"I was told two days, Master."

"May I have a blanket?"

"We left it behind."

"And my book?"

"In Bari."

"No money, no comfort, no hope," said Mangus. He sniffed and patted the sack he was sitting on. "We are impoverished, but I'm sitting on a fortune's worth of pepper. What are you sitting on?"

"Cloves."

"If we had food, we'd eat a flavorsome meal."

"Master, people say the most nourishing food is hope."

"Hope," said Mangus, "is a menu on an empty plate. How will we be able to survive in Venice without money?"

"I'll think of something," I said, though I had no idea what that something might be.

"It was foolish to have come," said Mangus. "I'm too old for this."

"Does being older make you wiser, Master?"

"Fabrizio, the older I get, the more I know how little I know."

"But," I protested, "that would mean as you age, the more ignorant you become."

"'Tis true."

"Then babies are the wisest people in the world."

"Perhaps they are," Mangus replied. "All I know is that ignorance is the first step to knowledge."

"Then I shall study to realize my ignorance."

"Fabrizio, must you have an answer for every question?"

"Master, a good servant is never supposed to question his master, just answer."

Master sighed but said no more.

Restless, I got up. "I'll see if I can find some food," I said.

I went forward. In the prow was a small section where the ship's carpenter worked. Two other subdivisions held the ship's goods — bales and barrels of spices. Mangus and I were lodged in another section.

At the boat's stern was the capitano's cabin. Before that area was a room where food was cooked. I begged for some bread from the cook, then took the stale pieces I was given and returned to Mangus.

The bread relieved our hunger somewhat, and we settled into the dank, gloomy, and uncomfortable hold. Mangus eased himself upon the lumpy spice sacks, folded his hands across his stomach, closed his eyes, and gave way to silent thought.

I sat there listening to the tramp of feet overhead, the drumbeat, as well as the orders, which I did not understand. Not knowing what else to do, I crept out of the hold again.

Standing on the upper deck, I gazed upon the rising

and falling sea, with its constant roll of foam-edged waves that tumbled one over the other. The land was no longer in sight. But not so far away — like a school of fish — the other spice fleet galleys were moving with the pull of their own oars. I heard their officers shouting, calling, the slap of their oars, and the beat of drums.

As I looked at the other ships, I realized something: If it had been Rozetti who was stalking us, he might well be on one of the other ships, also heading for Venice.

Though I knew we needed to find that friar fast, I remembered what I had been told, that one hundred and eighty thousand people lived in Venice. I was unable to grasp what that might mean, except that to find *one* person in that vast population would be like seeking one grain of wheat from a whole sack.

Telling myself to be patient, I put my faith that as soon as we reached Venice I'd learn some useful magic. Yes, I told myself, Venetian magic would be the thing — the only thing — that could solve all our problems. I would put my trust in that.

CHAPTER 13

At dusk, though I saw no cities or towns, not a single candle flame, the galleys slowed. Then I heard multiple anchors splash down and all movement ceased. I could smell earth. We must have come close to land. Trumpets blew. Lamps were lit. The whole fleet — twenty galleys — lay at rest for the night.

Food was served, bread and fish. By the kindness of the cook, Mangus and I were fed. I borrowed bowls and an odd prong the cook called a "fork" — "from the Eastern empire," the cook claimed. So Mangus and I sat on spice sacks in the hold and poked at the food we had been given.

When we had finished eating, Mangus turned to me. "When we get to Venice, we'll need to find Brother Luca and his book as fast as possible. Have you any ideas on how we can locate him? I'm depending on you."

Not wishing to say I had not the slightest idea how to proceed, I said, "It sounds as if you are feeling ill, Master."

"I am."

"Just rest, Master. I'll return the bowls."

"You didn't answer my question: How are we going to find Brother Luca?"

"I promise I'll find a way," I assured him, only wishing I had an answer.

I brought the bowls and forks back to the cook. Wanting to avoid Master's hard questions, even as I tried to think of ways to find the friar, I wandered about the galley. Most of the exhausted rowers lay stretched out on their benches, sleeping where they had labored.

As I roamed, I came upon four men who had gathered in a tight circle, a broken oar blade on their knees. Stuck on the wood was a small candle. The men, their faces illuminated by the small flame, were playing cards while bantering among themselves. One of them I saw was Cardano, the rude man who had been with the galley capitano.

Having nothing better to do, I stood near and watched the men playing. It was a gambling game. Coins were laid down; cards were passed out and then put down one by one. The holder of the high card won and took the coins. Once a hand was over, the deck was mixed, and the cards were distributed again. A foolish game of chance.

As I looked on, I had a thought: King Claudio had told us that Brother Luca was well known in Venice. Since these men most likely came from Venice, they might know where the friar was.

Before I could speak, one of the men looked up. It was Signor Cardano. "Do you wish to play, boy?" he asked.

"With permission, Signore, I should like to, but I have no more money."

Cardano studied me for a long moment, then held out a few coins. "Now you have."

"Thank you, Signore," I said. Deciding this was his way of apologizing, I took the money and sat down.

When cards were dealt to me, I began to play, losing each hand as well as my money, to the amusement of the men.

Signor Cardano smiled. "You said before that your master was searching for books. I hope he does better than you do with cards."

The others laughed. Irritated by their disrespect, I said, "Have no worries about my master, Signori; he's a magician."

"Is he?" asked Cardano.

"With permission, he is."

"Is he good at it?" He was now paying close attention to all I said.

"Signore, I assure you, he's the most famous magician in the world."

"Since you are his servant," said Cardano, his voice full of mockery, "I suppose you must know magic, too."

"I do."

"Yet you have not won one hand in our game."

Feeling pressed to prove myself, I took up the next four cards that were dealt to me, rolled them over in my hands, and, with a flourish, made them disappear.

Taken aback, the men stared at me. I opened my hands to reveal the cards, unable to resist smiling.

Signor Cardano said, "Very well, how did you do that?"

"I told you, Signore, my master is a magician."

No one said anything. But the men's mood had changed. Though the game continued, they kept stealing glances at me, no one more so than Signor Cardano.

See, I thought with glee, *they are paying attention to me. As always, magic gains respect. Now is the time to ask them about Brother Luca.*

"Tell me, Signori," I began, "do you all come from Venice?"

The men said they did and began to talk among themselves about what they would do during their time at home.

As they talked, I felt pressure on my leg. When I looked down, I realized that Cardano was secretly giving me a card. *There*, I thought, *he's scared of me and wants to be on my good side.*

Without looking at the man, I took the card, played it, won the hand, and gained the money on the board.

Cardano said, "Tell me, boy, when I asked you before why your master has come to Venice, you said he was looking for books. Then you said he was a magician. Now, tell the truth, why has he really come to Venice?"

Deciding he wished to be my friend, I saw my opportunity. I said, "He's seeking someone, Signore."

"Who is that?" asked Cardano.

I hesitated. Maybe I should not say. I remembered the innkeeper's words: Informers — Black Robes, he had called them — were everywhere, even on ships. Did that explain why Cardano asked me to play? Had he given me money and cards so I would reveal what I had said, that Master was a magician and was looking for Brother Luca's book? What if this Signor Cardano was — as I had been warned — a government informer?

But I told myself, it would be so wonderful if we could find Pacioli quickly.

"With permission," I said. "Once in Venice, he needs to meet a Franciscan, a friar by the name of Luca Pacioli. Do you know of him? Where he might be found in Venice?"

"Why is your master seeking this particular friar?"

Feeling I had to answer, I said, "He's written a book that contains a secret method of making money."

That brought silence. No cards were played.

"Secret?" said Cardano. "Is that more of your magic?"

I looked around at the faces of the card players. They were grave.

"Perhaps you didn't know," one of them said. "But magic is illegal in Venice." As he spoke, his eyes shifted to Cardano, as if he were warning me about the man.

One of the other men said, "People who report illegal activities get big rewards."

It was as if I had received a punch on my chest. Wishing I had never spoken, I threw down my cards and snatched up the coins I'd won. In haste, I excused myself by saying I must attend my master.

Down below, I found Mangus stretched out on his sack of pepper. "Look, Master," I said, holding out my hands with the coins I had won. "We have money again."

"How did you get it?"

"Playing cards with the oarsmen."

"Cards? Did you do some of your tricks?"

"One of the rowers took pity on me."

"How did you help him?"

"I did nothing, Master."

"When money is taken, Fabrizio," said Mangus, "something is always given."

Not wishing to admit what I had revealed, I said nothing more. All the same, I was aware I might have put us in grave danger.

CHAPTER 14

WE SAT IN SILENCE UNTIL MANGUS SAID, "FABRIZIO, I fear there is something the matter with me."

"Is it the way ship slips and slides, Master?"

"I'm afraid it's more than that." Mangus became quiet for a while before saying, "We have not spoken about it, Fabrizio, but if something happens to me — if I die — you will need to get back to Pergamontio and tell Mistress Sophia. She must not be ignorant of my fate."

Alarmed, I gazed at Mangus. His eyes were half-lidded. His fingers trembled slightly. It was a reminder of how old and frail he was. Yes, we were going to Venice, which was what *I* had wanted. But what if he became seriously ill? If he died? What would I do?

Nothing. All I could do was pray he would get better.

But the following day as we continued northward, Master told me he was feeling worse. Increasingly uneasy, I put all my faith in the idea that as soon as we reached Venice, I'd learn some magic that could help him.

I did make sure to avoid the rowers with whom I had

played cards the night before. I worried most about the one named Cardano and whether he would keep what I'd told him — Master's magic — to himself. But there was nothing I could do about my folly. Instead, all that day I stayed close to Mangus. The old man said almost nothing. The kind of playful banter he and I loved to share was gone. With each of us wanting the voyage to be over, we waited in impatient silence. The crash of the oars — the beat of the drum — became our measure of time. Tedium became our tempo.

As midday came, I realized we were going slower and the air had grown dank. I went on deck and saw that a gray mist had settled about us, cold, clotted, and moist, so dense the galley fleet seemed to be sliding through a sea of soup. I recalled Father Ambrose telling me that God kept the sun from Venice. Did the murk, I wondered, mean we were nearing the city?

I was just able to see a few islands that appeared to be nothing but tall grasses. On some of the islands, there were buildings. Were they monasteries? Brother Luca was a friar. Did he live on one of those islands?

I caught glimpses of a few people bending over what had to be shallow water. As I continued to watch, I saw — through the miasma — what appeared to be high ridges. Puzzled, I stared. No one had mentioned mountains near Venice.

Small boats emerged out of the fog. One of them came alongside our galley. A man stepped from one such boat and came aboard. I saw it happening on the other ships.

The man who came onto our ship went to the rear deck and greeted the capitano. Then the new man began to give orders to those who worked the rudder.

I soon understood why. Under the guidance of the man who had just come aboard, our galley threaded her way through a multitude of tight channels, small, low islands and marshes.

As the fog thinned, I realized it was not mountains I had seen but a line of jagged roofs crowded one upon the other, along with a multitude of lofty towers poking into the leaden sky.

I was seeing a city.

Now the whole fleet — in one long row — our galley,

as before, the last in line, maneuvered to enter a wide river. The water was dark, dirty, and foul-smelling. Squawking pigeons and seagulls swooped through the air, snatching bits from the water.

In the river were numerous small sleek boats that darted about like a school of fish. Black in color, long and low, they were propelled by single rowers standing on skinny sterns.

A deck officer came up to me and must have noticed what I was looking at. "Gondolas," he said, pointing to those slim boats. "Those bigger ones with a square sail are called *battelli.* That one with the colored sails, a *topo.* Fishing boats." He pointed to a boat with several rowers. "*Caroline.* For hauling goods."

On either side of the river, along the shore, were multiple black poles looking like fingers poking out from the water. Small boats were tied to them. I began to see countless buildings, among them houses made of brick and stone, between three and five stories high.

We were approaching the city.

As the fleet drew closer, just as in Bari, church bells

began to ring. Trumpets blared. On the shores, I saw people cheering. Venetians were welcoming their spice fleet. My eagerness grew in equal measure.

I hurried down to Mangus. With my assistance, he got up sluggishly. Hearing him breathe with effort, I sensed his health had grown worse. With care, I guided the old man to the top deck.

As our galley drew up to a landing — the last of our fleet — I saw, through a thin curtain of wet gray haze, two tall columns. Atop the column on the left, a man was standing on what appeared to be a dragon. On top of the column to the right stood a gigantic lion with *wings.*

A lion with wings!

Absolutely thrilled, I gawked at the animal. The thought *Everything I've been told about the city is true!* filled my mind with glee. Worries fled. My heart thrummed. All would be well. Better than well. I was about to become a true magician. The first thing I'd do was make Mangus healthier. Because I had no doubt, we had reached Venice, the city of magic.

CHAPTER 15

But as I continued to gaze up at the winged lion, I gradually realized it was not a real, living beast; it was a statue made of stone. The lion's parts — head, wings, tail — were held together by metal brackets. I turned to the other column. It was the same: not a real person standing on a dragon but another statue.

One moment I had been telling myself that the marvels of Venice I'd been told about were all true. Now I was filled with doubt and disappointment.

Let it be said: Nothing is more shocking than what is real.

But I had no time to deal with such discouraging thoughts. The rowing drum stopped beating with one final, thunderous thump. With a harsh jolt, our ship bumped against a stone embankment, shuddered, was secured with ropes, and then stopped.

No sooner did our ship cease to move than boarding planks were flung out from the landing. A lowering, cold mist swirled about us, making it hard to see. But I certainly saw men garbed in black or red robes march aboard. Pale hands — like bird claws — poked out from full sleeves. When these men began to give orders, I decided they must be government officials.

Sure enough, the black-robed men started to examine the cargo our galley had brought, every bale, bundle, and box. At the same time, the red-robed men wrote down the information in a small tablet. Abacuses clicked like summer crickets. Were these men tax collectors? Were they using that secret bookkeeping method?

I was tempted to ask them to explain what they were doing but, nervous it might be forbidden, I didn't dare. Instead, Mangus and I remained on the galley's deck and watched, uncertain what to do. It wasn't long before two men, one black-robed, the other red-robed, approached us.

"You," the black-robed one said to Mangus. "Who are you and why have you come to Venice?"

I had no idea how the man knew we were strangers. Nor what his authority might be. My first worry was that Cardano told him what I'd said about Mangus being a magician.

"With permission, Signore," I answered right away, "my master is a trader."

"In what does he trade?"

"Books," I said, deciding it best to repeat what I'd said before.

"What's your master's name? Where are you from?"

"Mangus. Of Pergamontio."

"Where is that?"

"Italy."

The red-robed man wrote my answers in his book.

Scowling, the black-robed man grabbed my arm, twisted me around, and said, "Do you see that building?"

He was pointing to an immense structure bigger than I had ever seen that faced the water along where our galley and other galleys lay. Along the building's extraordinary length were multiple tiers of arches, columns, windows, sculptures, and balconies, all pale pink. Hanging from the balconies were scarlet flags, which bore images of golden lions with wings. The fluttering flags made it appear as if the beasts were flying.

"With permission, Signore, I do see. But what is it?"

"The Doges' Palazzo."

"The doge, Signore?"

"Agostino Barbarigo, the elected head of the Most Serene State of Venice. Take heed: His palazzo is full of prisons with foreigners who break our laws. And mind: Our punishments are harsh — strangulation or drowning."

Forcing me to turn about, the Black Robe pointed to someone who appeared to be sitting at the base of one of those columns.

"Do you see that man?" he said.

"The sleeping one?" I replied. He was easy to see because, although hundreds of men were milling about, they avoided that spot.

"He's not sleeping. He's dead. Executed for breaking our laws."

I stared with revulsion.

"Now get yourselves ashore." The man shoved me away as if I were something dirty.

Knowing we were there to steal that friar's book, I was unnerved. Mangus said nothing. I was not even sure he had heard what the official said or noticed the dead man.

All he said was "Fabrizio, I need to get off this boat." You may be sure I agreed.

Leaning on my arm, Mangus allowed himself to be led so that we were caught in the crush of rowers pushing and shoving to get off our galley, then crowding onto the landing area.

As soon as we stepped on land, I looked about in fear that someone would be there to waylay us. But the crush of people was so dense, and my vision so obscured, that we might have been watched but I would never have known.

I halted and scanned around. I thought I saw Cardano following us, but there were so many people, I wasn't sure. Worse, within moments, he was lost to my sight. I had to tell myself, *It's foolish to see enemies everywhere when in fact you see none.* Once again, I reminded myself of Mangus's words: "Eyes are for seeing, not guessing."

Even as I tried to reassure myself, Mangus squeezed my arm and murmured, "Get me away from these crowds." His breathing was labored. He looked ill.

"Yes, Master," I said. "I'll do my best. I just need to make sure that we aren't being spied on."

"Are we?"

"I can't tell, Master. There are so many people."

"Dear Lord . . ." Mangus muttered.

I rebuked myself anew for revealing the reason for our being in Venice to Signor Cardano. In haste, I reminded myself that the first thing I must do was find safe shelter for my master. Accordingly, I began to work our way through the crowds. As I went forward, I saw a colossal brick tower, taller than any structure I had ever seen, its top so high it melted into the mist. No doubt, from its lofty summit I'd see the entire world.

But before I made sense of the tower, I saw a gigantic church topped by a cross, a building far larger and grander than Pergamontio's cathedral. In contrast to the thick cloud of mist that filled the air, the building glittered with multiple towers, arches, domes, colored mosaics, and columns, everything glistening with more splendor and wealth than anything I'd ever seen before, more like a fantastical dream than something real. Indeed, atop the church's entrance stood four giant horses, looking as if they were ready to leap forward and trample the world.

I turned to Mangus in hopes he might explain, but the old man was gazing at the church with his own look of openmouthed wonder.

Wishing to get away, I moved us forward into a vast open area far grander than any city space I had ever witnessed. If its purpose was to make a person feel small, it did so to me.

Thousands of people were milling about. It seemed as if the entire world's population had gathered. Some were assembled in small groups. Others stood alone. Many of the men wore robes. And considerable numbers wore masks.

Masks!

Then *some* of what I was told about Venice was true.

For the most part, these masks were simple white ones that covered eyes. Many others were elaborate, shaped and painted to resemble large animals. Other masks were birdlike in shape, with sharp protruding beaks.

The robes these masked men wore were most often red or black. Small black caps were on their heads. Other masked men wore sumptuous clothing, doublets, and bright leggings, with fine leather shoes and boots. Some wore elegant capes that covered their shoulders, heads crowned by large, round hats. Some had swords.

The women I saw were also masked but with black masks. Dressed in multicolored gowns, they showed their long hair, while their heads were covered by caps or shawls, faces concealed so just eyes peeked out. High wooden shoes lifted them off the ground.

Amid this display of rainbow-colored wealth, it was a relief to notice poorer folk, garbed in ordinary clothes, some in rags. Not masked, they darted about the crowd like drab minnows among the flashier fish.

As I stood there, looking with amazement, trying to make sense of it all — and failing — I saw a lengthy procession of white-robed priests and black-gowned nuns — not masked — surely more religious folk than existed in all Pergamontio. Holding lit candles in hand and chanting in solemn unison, they sounded like a moaning wind. As they proceeded into that immense church, no one seemed to take notice of them other than to move aside.

Then I saw a group of men whose unmasked faces bore long black beards. They wore robes covered with colorful embroidery, along with pointy black slippers on their feet and high white turbans on their heads. From their wide leather belts hung curved swords.

Next, I saw a man dressed in a baggy blue suit, his face covered by a red mask. As I observed him, he threw five balls into the air and kept them rotating there.

That had to be magic.

As Mangus and I — ever more bewildered — meandered about, I saw many flimsy booths had been erected for the selling of goods: fine glassware with glass as clear as the sky, leather goods, lace, pots of spices, bolts of multicolored silk, white wax candles as well as weapons, all for sale — an array of goods both fabulous and luxurious.

There were also dealers (sometimes masked) of food, bread, vegetables, meat, and fish. Some of the things they sold — like golden balls, which I saw people put to their mouths and eat — were unknown to me.

And more wonders.

I saw a man playing with big snakes.

I saw musicians making music on instruments I was unable to name.

I saw somebody striding about on long poles.

One man had a small table set before him, upon which he moved small cups. Others tried to guess if there were balls under the cups. I watched: People never guessed right.

That, too, had to be magic.

Not far from him, I saw a woman pull bright scarfs from a hat where there had been no scarfs. More magic.

Over, under, and all about, a gray mist moved about us like a thin silk veil, making the world even more fantastic.

Baffled and bedazzled, I continued to roam about, gawping upon one sensation after another. How, I asked myself, in all this confusion was I ever to find one book?

It had turned colder. Night was coming. I kept moving in the hope I might see something, anything, that would suggest a place for Mangus to rest. The more we walked, the more anxious I grew that lodging would not be found.

Out of nowhere, I felt a tug on my tunic, followed by a voice: "Boy? Are you looking for a place to stay?"

I spun about.

The girl who had spoken was short enough so that I had to look slightly down at her face, which was smeared with dirt. Tangled dark red hair reached her shoulders. Her tunic was ragged, her feet, despite the chill, bare. She was skinny, with thin arms and small hands, making her seem something spiderish. She looked at me in a way that suggested her question wasn't to be denied.

The girl repeated what she had said: "*Do* you want a place to stay, boy?"

Since I didn't think Mangus noticed the girl, I made my own quick decision: "If you take us to a decent place," I said, "I'll pay you."

"Follow me," she said, giving my arm another tug before walking away.

"Master," I said. "This girl says she will take us to lodging."

When Mangus made no objection, I began to follow the girl while wondering who she was. The next moment, remembering what had happened to me in Bari, I thought: *What if this girl is working for our enemies and leading me into a trap?*

Unsure what to do, I halted.

CHAPTER 16

THE GIRL ALSO STOPPED. "ARE YOU COMING OR NOT?" she demanded in an urgent voice. Not wanting to show my unease, I replied, "Why are all these people wearing masks?"

The look on her face suggested I was very ignorant. "What do you think? It's carnival."

"What's carnival?"

"Where do you come from that you don't know?"

Determined not to give anything away again, I just shook my head.

"Carnival is the celebration before Lent. It goes on for a few more days. The masks? Venetians love two things: money and secrets."

Still stalling, I waved my hand: "What do you call this enormous place?"

The girl took a few steps, then paused to look back at me. "It's the Piazza San Marco," she said with obvious vexation. "Yes? No? Do you want lodging? I can find someone else."

I glanced at Mangus. He looked back, eyes pleading for rest.

"Go on," I called to the girl. "We'll follow."

She started off again but kept looking around to make sure we were following. She must have realized Mangus was unable to walk fast, because she slowed down. Once again, I sensed that our going was important to her. I was unable to imagine why.

We went out of that gigantic piazza by moving between two buildings, into a slim slit of an alley, which I never would have noticed on my own. *This can't be a true street*, I told myself as I continued to trail after the girl, wondering where she was taking us.

Though the passageway was thin, it was packed with people (many masked) moving both ways. It was so crowded that Mangus and I were forever stepping aside, turning shoulders, squeezing against walls, bumped and elbowed, letting others pass, while saying, "With permission . . . Excuse me . . . Sorry . . ."

Jostled, I was spun around, and that's when I saw a man in a black robe some ways behind us. I stopped and stared — *Was he following us?* — but I was bumped again. When I looked a second time the person was gone.

All the same, I gripped Mangus's arm tighter and tried to move faster, while attempting to see where we were going. I was glad the girl had red hair. As we went along, I kept glancing back, but to my confusion, there were many black-robed men. Surely, they weren't all following us.

Tiny shops lined the streets: a vegetable store, a seller of glass beads, a mask shop, a bakery, among others. Hungry, I wished we had paused, but the girl didn't stop.

The next moment, we stepped out of the lane and found ourselves on the edge of water. My first thought was that we'd come to a river, but this was unlike any river I had ever seen.

No more than fifty feet wide, it carried a green-tinted flow between sharp embankments of pitted brick. When I looked up and down, I saw the water splitting into other streams.

"Hey!" I called.

She stopped and looked back.

"What's this?" I pointed to the water.

She looked astonished by the question. "What do you think?" she said. "It's just a canal. Venice has hundreds of them."

The canal was almost as crowded as the lanes upon which we had walked, but instead of people, it swarmed with small boats, low in the water with high prows and sterns, the same skinny black ones I had seen when we first approached the city. The rowers of these boats stood in the stern, working a long oar. They wore colorful jackets, tight leggings, and caps, some of which had feathers.

On both sides of the canal stood brick, wood, and stone buildings — tight, one against another — that rose three, four stories high. The waters of the canal lapped their doorways and entry risers as if one were supposed to step right into the canal water or out of it. In fact, it was hard to say where the water ended and the buildings began. Where water and stone met, green slime coated all, making it difficult to know what was solid and what was liquid. It was as if the buildings were living things growing right out of the canal.

Then, too, some of the buildings were covered with

what looked to be elegant white lace, some kind of facade — *more masks*, I thought, though I quickly grasped that these facades were made of stone.

And there were lines of multicolored laundry — shirts, trousers, and whatnot — hung, flag-like, on lines that draped from window to window, which told me people lived in these houses.

By way of contrast, on rooftops, I saw a forest of chimneys with bulging tops, which made me think of huge mushrooms.

"Come on," the girl called to me. I had been standing there trying to make sense of what I was seeing.

Clinging to my master's arm, I moved along the stone-paved walkway that ran along the canal's edge. With so many people rushing by, I was aware that one bump would throw me — and Mangus — into the water, where we would probably drown.

The girl, who kept glancing back, reached a flimsy-looking wooden bridge that arched high across the canal. I followed, leading Mangus by the hand. When I reached the highest point of the bridge, I turned around to help my master up. That was when I saw another black-robed man behind us.

Was it the same man or a different one? Was he following us?

No sooner did I see him than he was lost among the crowds. I glanced at Master to make sure he was safe. He was, though looking worse.

You're seeing enemies everywhere, I scolded myself. *It's because this place is so strange and there are so many people.* I reminded myself that my task was to get Mangus to wherever the girl was taking us.

We got over the bridge and headed into another brick-lined alley. This one was so narrow I was able to reach out and touch the right and left walls at the same time. Even so, it was just as crammed with masked people.

The next moment, we popped out of it, made a turn, and then went to another alley. We kept on, turn after turn, alley after alley, canal after canal. It was like a maze, so I had no idea where we were going.

Mangus came to a complete stop and gripped my arm. In a croaky, breathless voice, he said, "I can't . . . go anymore." He leaned against the alley wall where we were and closed his eyes.

"Please, wait," I called.

The girl stopped and looked back.

"My master is ill. How much farther is it?"

"Close."

"Lean on me," I said to Mangus, and put my arm around him. He was wobbly. That awful thought came back into my head: *What if he dies?*

Not knowing what else to do, we continued along more lanes, more turns and canals, Mangus taking little more than baby steps. To make things worse, it was growing darker.

To my enormous relief, the girl finally called, "We're here."

CHAPTER 17

I GUIDED MANGUS INTO WHAT PROVED TO BE A covered walkway, its roof so low that Mangus had to stoop to pass through. We moved in a single file, the girl, me, and then Mangus, the old man's hands on my shoulders as I led him forward.

Once we passed through the dreary passageway, we stepped into a small campo, an open courtyard. A few candle lamps on decaying walls shed a little light, giving fuzzy illumination to a thin, shredded mist that lay over the stone tiles like a frayed, floating blanket.

Around the courtyard — from what I saw — were dilapidated brick buildings several stories high with lop-sided doors, broken windows, and sagging balconies. Nothing was level. In the middle of the campo was a low white circular stone capped by a wooden lid from which a large lock dangled. The whole area was deso-late save a scruffy gray cat, which lay sleeping, head between its paws, a sure omen, I knew, of coming storms.

The girl led us to one of the lower doors and opened it on its leather hinges. She went in. I remained on the threshold, unsure about going farther.

"What is this?" I asked.

"It's where I live," said the girl. "It belongs to the Galley Rowers Guild."

"Are you a galley rower?"

Ignoring my question, she said, "Do you wish to stay? I need to know." She went to a table, took up a flint box, struck a spark with a fire striker, and lit a stumpy candle, bringing forth a small yellow flame.

It was a tiny, gloomy, and clammy room. Walls were cracked and clotted with spiderwebs. The wooden floor was uneven. There was a low rope bed — no blanket — a small table, a lopsided chair, and an empty bucket. On the table, a small book lay beside a pot of ink, a feather pen, and a large key sitting on a small box.

Recalling the Bari storeroom in which I had been trapped, I remained by the entrance, unsure what to do. I was relieved to see no lock or hasp on the door. *Then why does she have that key?* I wondered.

The girl gestured toward the bed. "The old man can rest there."

Mangus had already staggered into it, too fatigued to speak.

"Who lives here?" I asked the girl.

"Me."

"Who else?"

"No one."

"Where are your parents?"

"I'll ask the questions," she said, speaking bluntly. She nodded toward Mangus. "Is he your father?"

"He's my master. I'm an orphan."

"No mother?"

I shook my head.

She studied me for a long moment — as if what I said was important — then went to the doorway, leaned against the frame, and looked out. She appeared to be doing nothing more than gazing into the campo, where night had come. I was sure something I said had upset her.

"How do you live?" I asked.

"I rent this room, work the prisons, and beg."

"A beggar, then."

"I need to live," she said, still not looking at me.

I said, "If we're here, where will you sleep?"

"On the floor. Will the room do?" she asked. There was tension in her voice.

I knew that Mangus was unable to go farther. But not certain about the girl, and wishing I knew more about her, I stalled for time. "Is there water to drink?"

"That round white thing in the center of the campo is a well. I have a bucket. But you'll have to wait till the priest unlocks it. He'll come soon." She turned about. "Staying here costs one lira a week." She held out a hand. "Yes? No? Make up your mind."

Feeling I had no choice, I offered a coin.

"What's your name?" I asked.

"Bianca. Yours?"

"Fabrizio."

Bianca took the money. Then she went to the table, picked up her pen, and wrote something in that book. *Was it my name?* I wondered with unease. The red-robed official on the galley had also put down our names.

"How long will you remain?"

"Not long, I hope."

She closed her book and put the pen down. I remained near Mangus, who lay quietly on the bed. His eyes were closed, his hands clasped over his chest. His rasping breath seemed to take a struggle. Anxious, I bent over him. "Are you so ill, Master?"

His wispy beard bobbed.

"Master," I said, as much to reassure myself as him, "don't worry. I'll take care of you."

Fears spun through my head: Here we were in a strange and packed city. If we had been followed, our enemies knew where we were. And who was this girl? Should I trust her? Though I wanted to, I wasn't sure. Were we in danger? How were we ever to find that book by Brother Luca?

In other words, though we had finally arrived in the magical city of Venice, I had countless questions and not one answer.

CHAPTER 18

MY TROUBLED THOUGHTS WERE INTERRUPTED BY Bianca, who said, "You're not from Venice."

"How do you know?"

"You looked confused when I found you. Foreigners always look that way when they come here. Where are you from?"

"Pergamontio."

"Where is that?"

"Italy."

"I don't know anything about that. Why did you come here?"

"My master needs . . . a book. A book about money."

Bianca shrugged. "Venice. Money. It's the same word." She continued to stare out the door.

I turned back to Mangus and tried to think about how to help him. To Bianca, I called, "I need to get him some food."

She stepped away from the door. "Have any money?"

"A bit."

"Come on, then."

"Where?"

"To food. It's not far."

"Will my master be safe?"

"He's an old man. Who would trouble him?"

"Can you shut the door?"

The girl lifted a dismissive hand as if to say, "Why bother?"

I bent over Mangus. "Master, I'm going to get something for you to eat." Though not sure he heard me, I said, "I'll be back as fast as I can."

He made no response, and I went outside.

Since we had arrived, some fifteen women had gathered in the campo around that center well. A gray-robed priest was unlocking the well lid. Across the top of the well lay a bar from which wooden buckets, attached by ropes, dangled. As the priest left, women began to draw up water.

I shut the door to Bianca's room behind me. Since there was no lock, I pulled it tight.

The girl had gone ahead and was talking to one of the women by the well. As I approached, I heard Bianca say, "I have an old foreigner and his servant boy staying with me."

The woman glanced at me with slight curiosity.

When I joined them, Bianca broke off her conversation and headed for the covered entryway. I followed. "What was that book you had?" I called after her.

"My account book."

Not wishing to show my ignorance, I said no more.

Once beyond the tunnel, she continued to lead the way but paid no attention to me. That was fine since I was trying to memorize the route we were taking so I'd be able to get back to Mangus on my own. Just in case.

We went along twisty alleys, over a canal, and then onto a different campo. The mist had clotted and settled over the open space. Scanty light leaked from small shops, with lamps flaring just inside their doorways. Unlike that gigantic piazza where we had first come, just a few people were lounging about. None wore masks.

To one side of the campo, I saw a church, whose twin towers rose and dissolved into the darkness. The church had a multicolored glowing window that looked like a gigantic flower. As we stepped into the campo, bells began to ring. I assumed it was for mass. Sure enough, a few people emerged from the mist and moved toward the church.

"What kind of food do you want?" Bianca asked.

"Anything. Bread. Some meat."

"This way."

As we went by the side of the church, I stopped and stared. Embedded in the wall was a stone head of a lion. Its fanged mouth, as if waiting to be fed, was a large hole.

"What's that?" I asked, pointing.

"The lion's mouth. Every section has one. It's so you can denounce someone. You write the person's name on a paper and put it into the mouth. The authorities will investigate. If the person is guilty, they'll be punished. And the one who made the accusation gets a big reward."

"Is that true?"

Bianca nodded. "But you have to sign your name. Because if your denunciation is false, it's you who will be punished. That's the way it is in Venice."

I recalled that advocate — Signor Cucinello — in Pergamontio telling me that in Venice the judges were lions. "Are there real lions in Venice?" I asked.

"I never saw one," said Bianca. "Just pictures of lions

on flags. And sculptures everywhere. The lion is the symbol of Saint Marco. Our patron saint. Here's a bakery."

I went into the small, softly lit store, which was like the bakeries in Pergamontio. Round loaves of crusty bread were stacked upon each other. I took one up and paid for it.

"Don't you want food?" I asked Bianca when I rejoined her outside.

"I'll share yours," she replied.

Impatient to return to Mangus, I said, "Never mind meat. I have to get back to my master."

Wanting to show I didn't need her, I hurried along the way we had taken. She walked behind as if to test me. "If you know nothing about Venice, why did you come here?" she called out from behind.

I ignored her.

Full night had arrived, the only light coming from lamps hanging from the sides of buildings, so that I moved from bubbles of brightness, then back again into clotted darkness. The air was so foggy, it made haloes around the lamps and dampened my face.

Eager to get back to Mangus, I walked faster, hurrying

along the edge of yet another canal. I didn't see the water, but I could hear it ripple and slosh below me. In the gloom, I noticed some of those long, slim boats pass by, looking like floating shadows.

A man, robed in black, head down, hurried by. As he went past, he reached out and gave me a push, sending me teetering on the edge of the canal.

Bianca, right behind, yanked me back to safety.

Heart pounding, I stood there, trying to hold down my fright. I twisted about, trying to see who had tried to drown me. Whoever it was had vanished. Bianca, smiling, was looking at me as if what had happened was funny.

"You need to look where you're going," she said. "Here, you're always by canals. If you're afraid," she added, "walk by my side."

"Someone pushed me," I said, my heart still thumping.

"Don't be silly. In Venice, there are rules. Your superior walks near the walls. You are nobody's superior, so you need to walk by the canal edge. But be careful."

I didn't reply, but I had no doubt, our enemies were

ready to pounce. Had pounced. Who, I wondered, had pushed me?

"Are you going to just stand there?" said Bianca. She started off before I could reply. I hurried after her.

"Why would anyone want to drown you?" Bianca asked after we had gone a bit farther.

Not willing to explain, all I said was "Are we close?"

"You didn't answer," she said.

"I don't want to."

"What are you afraid of? Is it that — what did you say — that money book you're after?"

I kept my mouth shut.

She gave me an irritated look but led us on through the covered entryway into her campo. The well lid had been relocked, but a couple of women remained by the well, talking to one another in low voices.

It was only as we approached Bianca's room that I realized the door was open. Remembering that I had closed it, I rushed inside and looked about.

Mangus was not there.

CHAPTER 19

All I could manage to say was "My master . . . he's gone."

"He must have gone for a walk," said Bianca.

"He can't," I said. "He's sick."

Frowning, Bianca stood staring at me, all the while twisting a strand of her red hair.

I bolted past her, went to the door, and looked out. The light in the campo was enough to see that Mangus wasn't there, just those two old women by the well.

"Ask them," I said, pointing.

"About what?"

"My master," I cried. "If they know what happened to him."

Bianca gave me an annoyed look. "Why are you so upset? Old men wander." She tapped her head to suggest such people had weak minds. "He can't be far," she added.

"Please, ask."

Giving me a dirty look, Bianca went off across the court.

I flung the bread onto the table and followed.

"Signora Labora," Bianca called to one of the women. "An old man was staying in my room. This boy's master. He's gone, and we don't know where. Did you see him?"

The woman turned. Her face was full of distress. She looked at me, at the other woman who was there, and then back to Bianca. "Black Robes," she said in a low, upset voice. "Two of them. From the Council of Ten. Right after you left, they went to your door and led the old man away."

"Led him away?" I said with disbelief.

"They wanted to know where the boy went."

"Why?" said Bianca.

The woman spread her empty hands, as if to say, "I don't know." "And, Signora," she added in an undertone, "they asked for your name, too."

"Did you tell them?" Bianca asked, her voice now anxious.

"I had to. They threatened me."

"How long ago?" I asked.

"Not long."

I ran to the campo's entry and raced through. Once

beyond, I stood on the lane and looked both ways, trying to see through the mist. A wall torch with a small, fluttering flame provided scant light. Any number of people passed by. None were Mangus.

He was gone. Two men in black robes had taken him away. Hadn't the innkeeper in Bari warned me about them?

I remembered it was a government man in a black robe who had questioned us on the galley when we had first arrived. There were, I recalled, some who followed us. And it had been a man in a black robe who had tried to push me into the canal.

Bianca came out of the entryway. Soon as she did, I asked, "What is the Council of Ten?"

"They rule the city and meet in secret every day."

"Why would they take my master?"

"You know better than me," she said. "Maybe it's that book you said he came here for." Bianca's look was full of bemusement, as if I were a riddle. "Is that book important?"

Ignoring the question, I said, "That council: Are they the only people with black robes?"

"Of course not. Lots of people wear them."

"If it was that . . . council . . . what will they do to him?"

"Somebody must have accused your master of something. For the Black Robes to come so quickly, he must be important. If they arrested him, they'll question him and find out if he's guilty. If he is, he'll be punished. Maybe executed. That's what they do."

Into my head came the awful image of that dead man I had seen at the San Marco landing.

"He's done nothing," I insisted. "I'll go talk to the council."

She made a scornful sound. "It might not be them. And anyway, if it is them, no one can ask them anything. Not even the doge talks to the council."

"But why would they arrest my master?"

"*Is* that book illegal?"

Unwilling to reveal more, I said, "My master didn't *do* anything. We were just off the galley when we met you. You saw how ill he was."

She shrugged. "Then someone made an accusation against him."

"Where would they bring him?" I demanded.

"If it was the council's Black Robe who arrested him, he'd be taken to the prisons."

"Where are they?"

"The Doges' Palazzo."

"I need to go there." I was feeling desperate.

"You don't know anything, do you? It's night. You can't just walk into the prisons. They are locked. Besides, the curfew bell rings at midnight. I don't want trouble. You must have heard; they asked for my name, too. Helping you might make my life a lot more difficult than it already is."

"You are no help," I said.

"More than you," she said. "You're trouble. You can have your money back. I don't want it. Go away."

With that, she turned about and walked back into the entry, leaving me alone.

From behind shuttered windows came stabs of light. Music floated from somewhere. The smell of cooking was strong. The salt-tinged air seemed to seep inside me. Any number of people rushed by. I remained where I was, desperately scanning the shadowy, narrow street in hopes I'd see Master. But there wasn't the slightest hint of him.

Bianca said he might have been taken to the prisons in that building on the piazza. But I knew I'd be unable to make my way through the tangle of city alleys and canals on my own. I had to get her to take me.

I ran back into the campo and caught up with her as she was about to go into her room. "I need your help."

Ignoring me, she went inside.

I trailed after her. "Please."

"You said I'm no help," she said.

"I'm sorry. I'm upset. He's an old man. Sick. I have to take care of him."

Bianca glowered at me, went to her table, opened the small box, took out the coin I had given her, and held it out to me. She even reached for my hand and placed the money in it. My fingers curled around the coin. Then she picked up that book of hers, sat down on the bed, and made a show of reading it.

"A billion, billion begs," I said, holding out the coin.

"Take me to the prisons so I can find him. He's like a father to me. I'll give you double coins."

"I need to know," returned Bianca without looking up, "why you came to Venice. There must be some explanation for why your master was arrested. When Black Robes take a person, it's for a reason. And it's very bad that they asked about me. That means I'm in trouble, too. Unless you tell me the real purpose you came here, you need to go away."

Realizing I had no choice but to trust her, I took a deep breath. "My master needs to find a book written by a mathematician whose name is Brother Luca Pacioli. He's a Franciscan friar. There it is," I said. "That's why we're here. To find that book. Now please, take me to the prisons."

She frowned. "I told you: You won't be able to get in. Not during the daytime. And if you did find a way, there are so many prison cells, you still won't find him. But I know the prisons. So I'm the only one who can help you. Give me some bread."

I snatched up the whole loaf and tossed it to her.

She put her book aside and ripped off a chunk of bread and gobbled it down. It was obvious she was hungry.

"Why do you know the prisons?" I asked.

"Before I tell you, I must know more about why you came here. Why should the Black Robes try to kill you when you're just a foolish boy? It can't just be mathematics. Is your master a spy? Venice is full of spies. They come from everywhere. Are you trying to steal something? Learn how to make clear glass? How we build our galleys so fast? How to print books? The best way to make lace? Black Robes don't play games. Tell me everything or you can find your master for yourself."

I didn't know what to say. I had already told her the truth. It wasn't enough. I realized I'd have to say more to get her help.

"All right," I said. "I'll tell you. The reason we came here is — I wanted to learn magic."

She was about to eat another piece of bread. At the word *magic*, she lowered her hand. "Magic? What magic?"

"The magic in Venice."

"Who told you Venice had magic?"

"The king of Pergamontio."

"We don't have kings in Venice. We have a doge."

My hopelessness was only growing. "All right. If you must know, I'm a magician."

She sniffed and ate some bread. "I don't believe you. Anyway, magic is against the law. I knew of somebody who was arrested for doing it. You know what they did to her?" She made a cutting line across her throat. *"Zzzit."*

I held up the coin. "Do you see this?"

"Of course."

I rubbed my hands together and made it look as if the money disappeared. Then I pulled it from my nose. Next, I held up the coin and made it seem as if I pushed it into my right ear, then pulled it out of the left ear.

Bianca, mouth open, stared at me and twisted a strand of her hair around a finger.

"See? I *am* a magician. And since you want to know, I think my master was arrested because he's the most famous magician in the world."

She just stared at me.

I picked up the key that lay on her table, made it change into that bent nail I had in my pocket.

"Hey, I need that!" she cried.

When I brought the key back, she grabbed it from my hand and studied me. "Those were just tricks," she said.

"Think what you want."

She considered me for a long moment. "If . . . if I take you to the prisons," she said, "will you teach me that magic? I can make money with it."

"I thought you said it was illegal."

"It is. But I'm poor. If I were able to do tricks like that, I'd go to San Marco and perform. Make a lot of money. Enough to keep me alive. If I take you to the prisons, you have to promise to teach me."

"Fine," I said with annoyance. "I will. Now let's go." I held out the coin again.

She snatched it, put it in her pocket, and stood up. "Take the food." Clutching the key in her hand, she blew out the candle and stalked out of the room.

"Where are you going?" I called after her.

"What you asked. To the prisons. And then you're going to teach me your tricks. If you don't, I'll turn you over to the Black Robes and get a reward that's a hundred times more than what you just gave me."

CHAPTER 20

I GRABBED THE REMAINING BREAD AND FOLLOWED her out of the room, across the empty campo, back through the entryway, and onto that ill-lit lane at the canal's edge. "Where are the prisons?" I asked.

"Where I met you. Piazza San Marco."

"My master never would have been able to walk that far."

"Gondola," she said.

"What's a gondola?" I said, forgetting I had been told.

She spun around and faced me. "For someone who says he knows magic, you are not very smart. Gondolas are the way Venetians move about." She resumed her walk, moving fast, not bothering to see if I was following.

I called out. "How do you know so much about these prisons?"

"I told you. I get work there."

"Doing what?"

"Helping people." She stopped. "Give me some more bread."

I gave her some, but not wanting her to eat it all, I stuffed a piece into my own mouth first.

"What was that book?" I asked as we resumed walking. "The one on your table? Can you read?"

"My father taught me."

I had never met a girl who read. Her account book, she had said, but I had no idea what kind of book that was.

It was a struggle to keep up with her, passing through lit-up spaces, then dark spots, trying to see how narrow the walkways were, how near to the canal edges I came. As far as I could tell, the city was made of shadows and water.

Upon reaching yet another canal bank, Bianca stopped. Though there was a lit lamp on a nearby wall, its burbling waters looked black.

Bianca put fingers into her mouth and blew a loud, piercing whistle. From somewhere in the darkness, an answering signal came. Within moments, a gondola, long, low, and black, glided into view. On the boat's stern was a gondolier with a long oar in his hands.

Though the light was dim, I saw that his slim face was

marked with age-etched wrinkles. His eyes were deep-set, under bushy gray eyebrows. He had a slight white stubble of a beard. But he was dressed like a young man, in a red jacket with gold tassels.

Bianca gestured to him. "This is Aswad, my father's best friend. Mine too. And my godfather. He used to be a fisherman in Egypt but knows the waters in and around Venice better than anyone. Before my father went away, he made Aswad swear he would look after me until he came back. He does."

"Are you going to become a gondolier?"

"They don't allow women."

"Bianca," the gondolier called as his boat slid up to where we were standing. "What's the matter? We haven't talked in three days. I've been worried about you."

"I've been at San Marco trying to rent my room. But we need to go there. Fast. Now."

"Has something bad happened?"

Bianca motioned to me. "I rented my room to this boy's master. But the Black Robes took him. Probably to the prisons."

"What did he do?" Aswad asked Bianca.

"He says his master is a magician. And that he's a magician, too."

Though the light was poor, I saw Aswad's eyes turn to me. As always, say the word *magic*, and people looked at me in a new way.

"Real magic?"

"Just tricks," said Bianca, then added, "But he's promised to teach me how to do them. I could perform them at San Marco."

"That's risky, Bianca," said Aswad sternly.

"Aswad, I need the money."

"Why did they come here?"

"Something to do with a money book. And that magic. But in Venice," Bianca went on, "he's just a foolish foreigner."

Aswad studied me suspiciously, rubbed his chin, and snorted. "For you, Bianca, for you. Get in."

Bianca slid into the boat. The first thing she did was kiss both her godfather's cheeks, which he returned. When I didn't move, she called up to me: "Are you coming or not?"

Uneasy, I sat on the canal's edge, my feet dangling. The gondolier held out a large hand. I grasped it and dropped down. When I did, the boat dipped and swayed. Skittish of falling into the water, I snatched for the sides.

Bianca laughed and sat down at the bottom of the boat, near her godfather. "He may know magic, but he doesn't know gondolas."

Aswad grinned.

Holding in my anger, I worked my way toward the bow, sat in the bottom of the boat, pulled up my legs, wrapped my arms about, and stared ahead. All I saw was canal water.

Standing at the stern, Aswad began to row, his oar twisting and bumping on a grooved post. As we slid forward, there was a continuous slushing sound. I sniffed. The canal water smelled. That said, sparkles of light lay scattered on the surface of the dark water, so it was as if we were moving through a star-filled sky.

Flaming torches by the side of the canal shed some light on buildings that rose into the darkness. White balconies looked like masks. Flags with pictures of flying lions hung everywhere. Now and again, I heard talk, laughter, shouts. I kept seeing statues of people. In the semi-dark, they looked like ghosts.

As other gondolas went by, the gondoliers called to one another.

"Good evening, Aswad." "Hello, Aswad." "Keep going."

We went on. Bianca continued to talk to Aswad in a muffled voice. Sitting up by the bow, I was unable to hear what they were saying. I didn't want to. My thoughts were all about Mangus. I kept remembering what the Black Robe on the galley told me about people arrested in Venice: "Our punishments are harsh," he had said. "Strangulation or drowning."

I wished the city did have flying lions. I would have liked nothing more than to find Mangus, gather him up, and fly him back to Pergamontio.

I tried to see where we were heading. It wasn't possible. Our gondola turned too many times. And after a while, all lights disappeared. There were no sounds other than the steady noise of Aswad's oar strokes.

After I don't know how long, the gondola came to a

jarring stop. I looked up. Hazy light revealed we had reached some stone steps, which — like everything else — seemed to rise out of the water. I had no idea where we were.

Bianca climbed onto the steps, turned to me, and said, "Piazza San Marco."

She offered a hand. Holding on to her, I scrambled onto a stone-paved surface. Mist, feeling like cold silk, wrapped around us.

"Aswad," Bianca called to the gondolier. He had remained with his boat. "Many thanks."

"Should I wait?"

"We can walk."

"Please, Bianca, the night is never safe. Be careful."

"We will."

With a swish of the oar, Aswad and his gondola were gone.

As my eyes adjusted to the low light, I made out two columns, one of which, I remembered, held the winged lion on top. We had come to the place where our galley from Bari first arrived, the vast piazza. To my disgust,

I saw the dead man propped up against one of the columns. I forced myself to look at him. He wasn't Mangus.

"Let's go," called Bianca. She began to walk away.

I trailed after her.

Scattered about the piazza were torches, lamps, and flares, which revealed a fair number of people still there, though fewer than before. Many were masked. Music was playing. Men and women were dancing. They looked like floating spirits.

It wasn't long before Bianca and I were standing before what I had been told was the Doges' Palazzo. Bianca gestured to it, taking in the whole building. "If your master is in prison, he's in there. Satisfied?"

Being so close, the palazzo seemed even bigger than when I first saw it. Despite its vast bulk, in the fluttering light the countless arches, rows of columns, and multiple lion flags all seemed to quiver, as if alive. "Is there a way to get in?"

"Use your magic."

"It won't work," I mumbled.

"In Venice, the real magic is money."

"Is that how you get in?"

"Venice keeps its prisons full. The prisoners need food and messages. I bring what's sent. Both ways. But I have a way in." She held up the key. "I do it for money, and you may be sure I keep careful accounts."

I showed her the few coins I had left. "Is that enough?"

She peered into my palm and shook her head. "Before, you made money disappear. Can you make it appear?"

I shook my head.

"No more tricks?" Knowing she was mocking me, I said nothing.

"We'll go in my way," she said, and resumed walking. I hurried to keep up.

We headed toward the palazzo, then veered to the left, toward what appeared to be a separate building at its far end where there was a wide entryway. Over it was a huge sculpture of a man kneeling before a giant winged lion. The lion had one of its paws on a book as if to say, "This is mine." It made me think of the book we were seeking.

Bianca said, "The regular entry is closed now. We're not supposed to go in this way, but we'll try."

We went along a walkway lined by white stone

columns. On a wall, I noticed one of those lion head sculptures, its mouth wide open, waiting, I supposed, to swallow denunciations. Perhaps someone had put Mangus's name in that mouth.

We approached a broad flight of stone steps that led up to the second level of the building. Its breadth was illuminated — near the bottom — by a solitary wall lamp. Walls about four feet in height had been constructed along both sides of the steps. The higher the steps went, the darker it became, as if ascending into the night.

At the foot of the stairs stood two soldiers. They had swords attached to their belts, metal breastplates over their chests, bindings covering calves and ankles. On their heads were cloth caps in which feathers were stuck. Each soldier held a long, sharp pike, upon which they were leaning. The slumping way they stood made them appear tired.

Bianca went right up to one of the men. "Hey, Nicola," she called, "we need to go inside."

"Get off with you, Bianca," said the soldier with a grin. They seemed to know each other. "You know it's closed."

While there was no anger or bluster, the soldier and his companion lowered their pikes, crossing them to create a barrier.

Bianca turned about. "Come on," she said to me, and walked away.

I caught up with her. "Are we giving up?"

"They need to think we're leaving."

"Are we?" I asked.

"Course not."

"Where are we going, then?"

"You'll see. Stay close."

"How do those soldiers know you?"

"Told you; I'm here often. It's my business."

After moving from the steps, Bianca made a sharp turn and moved down a long pathway boarded by columns. To our left was a large, empty courtyard.

She continued, first turning left and then right, encircling the entire enclosure. When she came to a halt, I realized we had now come to the far back of that stairway, a good distance from the first and lowest step. Two soldiers were standing at the foot of the steps. They were facing outward, their backs toward us.

"Keep watching those soldiers," she said. "With luck, they'll soon fall asleep."

"You sure?"

"It's late. It's what happens."

"I don't understand what we're doing."

"Look at the side of the steps. See how the stones fit together? The crevices between them? Fingerholds. Footholds. We can climb up. Those soldiers will never see us."

"What if they do?"

She shrugged. "They'll chase me away."

"Do you do this often?"

"All the time."

"You said it was difficult."

"For you. Not me."

"It's awfully dark."

She snorted. "For me, the dark is light enough."

I turned toward the two soldiers. I was not sure how long we waited before one of them, though still standing with his hand on the pike, bowed his head.

"See," said Bianca. "He's asleep. Wait some more."

I kept my eyes on the other soldier. It wasn't long before he, too, nodded off.

"Come on," Bianca said. "Make sure your hands are dry or else you'll slip." She wiped her hands across her smock, then reached up along the wall of the steps, found a crack, and hoisted herself up. Next, she wedged her bare toes into a lower cranny and climbed higher.

Imitating what she did, I stretched up and wedged my fingertips into a chink between some stones above my head. Finding a grip, I pulled and, despite the pain, moved up.

Bianca reached the top first by rolling over a wall that flanked the steps. Once there she turned, leaned back over the wall, reached down toward me, grabbed my wrists, and yanked. In a matter of seconds, we were both by the top step. Below, the soldiers continued to stand — asleep, I hoped. They seemed not to have noticed what had happened: that Bianca and I were now inside the Doges' Palazzo.

CHAPTER 21

"THIS WAY," SHE WHISPERED.

We walked along a balcony, passing a series of tall, closed doors. A faint glow came from the piazza below.

Stopping before an open door, Bianca pointed to a bay beyond. "The prisons."

There was just enough light for me to see walls of brick and a floor covered with stone slabs. After going forward a few yards, we reached a steep flight of steps. They led to yet another door, a huge wooden one with rusty iron hinges.

Propped up against the doorframe sat a man. His head was thrown back, his eyes closed, and his jumbled gray hair fell about his face. His snoring was deep and rasping. Drool leaked from his mouth. A wooden keg — its cork removed — lay at his feet. Around his neck was a chain to which a key was attached.

"Federico," said Bianca into my ear. "By night, he sleeps with wine. By day, he takes bribes."

After showing me the key she had brought — it looked

like the one hanging from Federico's neck — she went up the steps, stepped over the man's legs, and then fitted her key into the door's keyhole. She beckoned to me.

I followed, treading gingerly over Federico. He never moved. Following her hand gestures, Bianca and I leaned against the door and pushed. The door swung open silently. After making sure to shut it behind us, we went forward into another long passageway whose walls and floor was stone.

"There are twenty prison cells along here," said Bianca. "They all have names: the Chamber of the Night Lords, the Lion and Lioness, the Volcano, and —"

"I don't care about their names," I interrupted. "Where would they have put my master?"

"Hopefully not the Torture Room."

"The Torture Room!"

"Shhh. Let's try to find him."

On the right-hand wall were vague crisscrossing shadow patterns made by light coming from the opposite wall. As we moved farther along the corridor, I realized the light was coming from behind thick iron bars woven one over the other, basket style. When I looked between the bars, it was into an almost-bare room. A lamp with frail light dangled from a low ceiling. The smell of mold, vomit, and muck was strong. It took a moment for me to realize that five women were sleeping on the stone floor. Among them, two girls.

I turned to Bianca for an explanation.

"Prisoners," she said. "Pickpockets, crooks."

We continued along the walkway, passing a door made of what appeared to be all iron. Encased by gigantic bolts, bars, latches, it seemed impassable. "For the condemned," Bianca said.

We passed another barred window. I looked in. Eight men were on the floor, sleeping.

"Do you see your master?"

I studied the sleepers, then shook my head.

"Don't worry. There are more cells."

We went by seven more cells before we found Mangus. He was alone in the small room, lying still on a wooden pallet. I wasn't sure he was alive.

Bianca looked at me.

I nodded.

Once more, Bianca turned her key in the keyhole and pulled. When the door swung open, I went into the cell and knelt before Mangus. "Master," I whispered.

The old man stirred.

Feeling deep relief to see him move, I said, "Master, it's me, Fabrizio."

With effort, Mangus pushed himself up on an elbow and looked about uncertainly. His eyes were bleary, his beard ragged, his sparse hair a jumble. His wool robe appeared torn, and his feet were bare. Spittle dribbled from one side of his juddering lips. I was jolted by how broken-down he appeared.

"Fabrizio?" he said. His look and voice suggested he wasn't sure it was me.

I squeezed his arm. "Yes, Master. It's me. Right here."

"I'm so glad to see you," he said in his croaky voice. He took up one of my hands and enfolded it in both of his, lifted it, and with dry lips kissed it. That was something he'd never done before.

"Master, did they hurt you?"

"Thankfully, no. I'm tired and cold, but unharmed."

"Why did they arrest you?"

"Somehow, they've learned of my reputation for magic. I told them it wasn't true, that I have no real knowledge of magic. But, Fabrizio, how would they, so far from Pergamontio, come to such a notion?"

Knowing well what I had told Signor Cardano on the galley, I was too embarrassed to confess. I looked around to see if Bianca had heard. She was standing next to me.

"Master, what do they intend to do to you?"

"They haven't said."

"Are you ill?"

"I've been sleeping. A good thing. Sleep is God's medicine. And when they put me in here, they gave me some bread and water. Have they arrested you, too?"

"I'm still free, Master."

"How did you get in here?"

"Bianca — remember? The one with whom we are staying. She knows the prisons. She brought me."

Mangus looked up at Bianca. "Thank you, Signora. I'm grateful."

Bianca, staring, said nothing.

"Master, do you want me to stay with you?"

"Fabrizio," he said, "I think the best you can do is find that Brother Luca. If he's as famous in Venice as King Claudio claimed, he might be able to get me free. Yes, find that friar."

"I'll try, Master. I promise."

"Thank you."

I tried to think of something funny or clever to say to cheer him up. I was unable to. Instead, I shifted toward Bianca. She was still staring at Mangus. I said, "Can't we just walk out with him?"

"We'd all be caught and kept."

I turned back to Mangus. "Master, I'll do what you ask: find Brother Luca and return as soon as possible."

"Bless you. And, Fabrizio —"

"Yes, Master."

His voice broke. "Don't . . . abandon me. Please."

The words caused me deep pain. It was clear that he was utterly dependent on me. It made me realize something: The one reason he would act and speak so was because what he had always told me was true—*he knows no magic.* But I had told those people on the boat from Bari that he *was* a great magician. As I stood there, I realized the depth of my love for him, and the harm I'd done.

Unable to speak, I followed Bianca out of the cell. I knew one thing. It was up to us to save Mangus.

CHAPTER 22

WE LEFT THE DOGES' PALAZZO THE SAME WAY WE GOT in, stepping over the still-sleeping Federico, then moving along the murky corridors. Upon reaching the wide steps, we scrambled down the sides. The soldiers below had remained asleep and never noticed. Once again, we were on the vast Piazza San Marco.

It was darker. Fewer people were about. The space seemed bigger. *The longer I'm in Venice, the smaller I become*, I thought to myself.

Bianca said, "What do you want to do?"

"I have to find that Brother Luca."

"Any idea where?"

"In Venice."

"Don't you know anything else?"

"He's a Franciscan brother."

"And?"

"A magician."

"More magic. What else?"

"Nothing," I said, all too aware of my ignorance.

"There are hundreds of Franciscans in Venice. Is he in a church? A monastery? One of those begging priests?"

"He's a mathematician. He's written a book. I'm sure my master is in prison because people don't want him to get that book."

"I need to know: Is your master a true magician? I heard him say he wasn't."

"I truly thought he was. But maybe he isn't," I said, though it was hard to admit.

"Then what you showed me — just as I thought — were tricks, right?"

I nodded.

"But if you teach them to me, I can make money."

"Is that the reason you're being helpful?"

"I told you: If you know nothing about money, you know nothing about Venice."

"It seems rich enough."

"For the merchants in the Rialto. Not me. But those merchants taught me to keep careful accounts, so I know exactly how poor I am. For now, we can go to my room."

"What about my master?"

"There are more than two hundred printers in Venice," she said. "They say we print more books than anyone in the world. In the morning, we'll go to printing shops and ask if anyone knows anything about that book. You can describe it. That might lead us to your friar."

"Thank you," I said. It was a start.

"We'll begin searching in the morning. But remember, you must teach me those tricks."

Exhausted, I was happy to agree.

We started off. It was a struggle to keep close to Bianca, and once or twice, I almost lost her.

It seemed forever before she announced, "We're here." With that, she ducked into the now-familiar low entryway that led to her campo. I came right behind. I was all but walking in my sleep.

No sooner did she reach the entryway's end than she stopped, turned, and knocked into me, crying, "Black Robes. Run."

Behind me, I heard voices shouting, "Stop. Halt."

We ran out of the campo the way we had come in. "This way," she called, charging forward.

Running, I followed, saw her turn, and then plunged into a dark alley. In the mist, it was as if I was following a shade. The sound of pursuing steps pushed me on.

"They're close," Bianca called from the shadows as she darted into a new passageway.

I barely managed to stay with her.

"Drop down," she hissed. "Make yourself small. Stay still." She followed her own orders. I did the same, lying flat on cold stones in hopes the darkness would conceal us.

Within moments, I heard footfalls that stopped near the head of the lane where we lay. I shifted my head, trying to see something, anything that would tell me who was chasing us.

Faintly, I saw two people. They were standing at the head of the passageway, holding a lamp and talking in low voices. Since they were garbed in black capes with hoods, it was not possible to see their faces. Straining to listen, I caught the name "Fabrizio." I also heard "Bianca."

They knew us.

The lamp was thrust into the alley. As the light

increased, I peeked up. One of them yelled, "There they are."

"Run," cried Bianca, springing up and leaping away. I did the same, dashing to where I thought she was, but she moved so fast I could barely see her. I sensed we had broken free until she, at an ever-greater distance from me, turned into a new walkway. I followed. I didn't think she went more than thirty feet when she made another shift. I tore after her. Or thought I had. It took only a few steps to realize she was no longer in front of me.

I had lost her.

Panicky, I stood in place, staring into the shadows. I listened, too, trying to gain some hint where Bianca had gone. Other than my own rapid breathing, I heard nothing.

I was alone.

With a hint of light coming from somewhere — impossible to know where from — I could barely see the indistinct walls of buildings. All was still. Uncertain in what direction to move, I stifled my desire to call out, afraid it would bring my pursuers. Instead, I tried to guess where I was. But I had no idea.

The silence was shattered by the sound of steps pounding behind me. A light seemed to explode. "There he is!" someone shouted.

I flung myself away from the voice only to smash into a wall. Smarting, I backed off, tried to shake away my dizziness, and tore off into a new direction, but after a few more steps, I crashed into yet another wall.

Utterly muddled and with a million sparks in my head, I had no idea where to go but kept turning in circles.

Knowing I had to move somewhere, I staggered forward, holding my hands out before me, only to feel another wall. I turned yet again. Finding nothing, I decided I was in the clear and lunged forward with no real notion as to where I was going, only hoping I was getting away from my enemies, while wishing desperately that I knew where Bianca was.

With nothing to impede me, I continued to rush forward. The next moment, there was now *nothing* beneath my feet, either. For a second, I was flying through the air, only to come crashing down into freezing canal water, where I instantly began to sink.

CHAPTER 23

DESPERATE TO RISE FROM THE WATER, I FLAPPED MY arms and churned my legs. Momentarily, I went up only to sink anew. Thrashing, I moved higher, enough to clear my mouth and shout a clogged "Help!" then dropped. I was — and to my terror, knew it — drowning.

As I started to go down, I felt a grip on my arm. With a jerk, I was hauled up. Who had taken hold of me I had no idea. I only knew I was being pulled out of the water. I didn't resist.

I was dragged onto a canal bank, where I collapsed like a sodden sack of salt. Once there, I lay on my stomach, coughing, gagging, spewing water, struggling for breath, my whole body quaking.

Helpless, not wanting to see my enemies — because I was sure it was they who had pulled me out — I remained where I was until I was able to roll over. When I looked up through blurred and blinking eyes, I saw Aswad, Bianca's godfather, bending over me.

"In Venice," he said with a grim smile, "even the cats learn how to swim."

Bianca, a lit lamp in her hand, was peering down at me over his shoulder. "Are you alive?" she asked.

I don't know if I managed to nod before rolling back onto my belly and coughing up more water. My legs gave a violent twitch.

"You're lucky Aswad was near," I heard Bianca say. "You look like a wet rat." She reached down and wiped water from my face. "Did someone push you again?" she asked with a smile.

I managed to say, "What happened . . . to those people . . . who . . . were chasing us?"

"Gone," said Bianca.

"Did you see them?"

"Two men," said Aswad. "I took them by surprise and chased them away. My oar makes a good club."

"Black Robes," Bianca said to her godfather.

"The worst," he said.

I said, "You saved my life."

"Glad to. I do it often enough for Bianca."

After a few more minutes, during which I just lay there, Aswad extended a hand. "Here, stand." Doing most of the work, he helped me to my feet.

Dripping wet, cold, my legs weak, I looked around. In the bit of light made by Bianca's lamp, other than seeing we were on a canal embankment, I had no idea where we were. My teeth chattered.

"I think those people were trying to kill you," said Aswad.

"You must tell us why," added Bianca.

I took a deep breath. "I'll tell you more if there's a dry place we can go to. But not your room. They know to go there."

"Find a safe place," Aswad said to Bianca while taking her lamp. "I have to work, but call out to me if you need."

"Come on," Bianca said to me.

"Stay close to her," Aswad cautioned, and patted my shoulder. "I know the canals. She knows the alleys." He smiled. "Best stay with us."

I thanked Aswad profusely. He offered more hopeful words, exchanged some cheek kisses with Bianca, and then she and I started off. We didn't talk as she guided us to an open, isolated campo. A few small shop lights revealed its emptiness. At the far end was a modest church. From one wall a tiny lamp hung, its red flame providing a thumb of light.

Bianca approached one of the stone walls where a statue was set into it. I recognized Saint Antonio because of his special cross. Since the statue jutted out from the wall, there was a hollowed-out recess right below. We settled into the niche, sitting on the cold stone tiles, backs against the equally cold church wall.

"We'll be safe here," she said, sounding, for once, tired.

I looked out from where we were. A damp fog had seeped into the campo, enfolding everything. Distances melted. Straight lines turned limp. Buildings grew soft. I had the feeling that I'd come to another world, a confusing and dangerous one. I sensed Bianca had chosen the spot so that if anyone approached, we would see them coming.

Church bells began to toll the hour from high above. I counted. Midnight Mass. I reached into my wet pocket and found and squeezed my lucky piece of iron, the bent nail. Then I tried to regain some warmth by wrapping my arms around myself. I thought of Mangus and my heart hurt.

"What made you choose this place?" I asked.

Bianca said, "I come here often and pray."

"Not in the church?"

"I like to be alone with Saint Antonio. He finds what's lost."

"What have you lost?"

She hesitated before saying, "My father."

"Where is he?"

"On a voyage."

"How long has he been gone?"

"A year."

"No word?"

She shook her head.

As we sat there, me weak and cold, she silent, I sensed her sorrow. I felt something I never had before: powerless. Tears spilled down my face. I smeared them away only to realize Bianca was looking at me.

She said, "If I don't know who and what you and your master truly are, I can't help. You need to tell me. Honestly."

I rubbed a hand over my face, shut my eyes, and opened them. I lifted my shoulders. Left. Right. I twisted my head to loosen my neck. I flexed my hands. Anything to take the stiffness — and fright — out of my body, which still felt damp and sore. All the while, I was thinking about how to answer Bianca's question.

She's the only one who can help me, I told myself, and started to speak.

"I come from the little kingdom of Pergamontio. I didn't know my parents, and I became a beggar. I'm not sure how I survived. It was the City Corporation, wanting me off the streets, that bound me over to Mangus and his wife. To earn his living, Mangus performed magic.

"Anyway, they treated me well and I came to care for them. It was there I gained a deep desire to learn what I had thought was his magic. I believed he did real magic."

"Does he?" she asked.

I shook my head.

"First you said your master was a magician," said

Bianca. "Then you say he isn't. Next, you said those things you did were really magic, then you said they weren't. Why is magic so important to you?"

It took a moment for me to think of an answer. "Because . . . because with magic you can make something from nothing. And I have nothing. As people say, the less money you have in your pocket, the more money you have in your thoughts."

"I have nothing, either."

Feeling that we were more alike than I had known, I related how King Claudio sent us to Venice to get Brother Luca's book with its secret way to make money. He said the city was magical. I told her I wanted to come so I could learn magic.

I told her about Rozetti, and how he threatened me, and the other things he did. Then I shared my encounter with Cardano on the galley, and how I told him my master was a magician.

"Are they the ones coming after you?"

"I think so. And if I don't help Mangus, he'll die in prison, and that will be the end of me, too."

For a while Bianca said nothing. Then, to my surprise, she said, "Show me how you do that trick, the one with the coin." She held out the lira I had given her. I must have been slow to take it because she said, "If you don't show me, I'll throw you back into the canal."

Knowing she didn't really mean it, that she was only wanting to lighten my mood, I took the coin and went through the motions of the trick, the same one I did for Mistress Sophia.

"Show me again."

I did and then offered her the coin. She worked through the gestures, the first time clumsily, the second time better.

"It takes a lot of practice," I said.

She said, "I'm glad it's not true magic. I don't want to go to the Torture Room. As for who is after you, people say that Venice is divided into two: Half the citizens are informers spying on the other half, who are informers spying on them."

I nodded. "When the Black Robes came to your room looking for me, those women told them your name. Does that worry you?"

She gave her inevitable shrug and yawned. "I'm always watchful. I suppose the best thing you can do is what your master said — get to that friar and his book. Then go back to your kingdom."

"You told me you know about printing shops."

"There are many."

She lapsed into silence. She was staring into the mist.

I said, "Tell me about yourself."

She stayed quiet, twisting a strand of hair, and then fiddled with the coin again.

I said, "You must miss your father?"

"I do."

"You must be so worried about him."

She nodded. "I worry all the time. It's been so long. I fear for him." Her eyes glistened. "I don't know what will happen to me if he doesn't return."

"I can't help you with that, but I'll teach you more tricks."

She worked the coin again. "Was that better?"

"You're a natural."

She fiddled for a while and then said, "People always

talk about how many rich people there are in Venice. But there are many more beggars. Aswad says all people are beggars but only some people look like one. That's me. My father — who taught me to read and do numbers — is a galley rower. About a year ago, he went to a place called the Black Sea. There's been no word from the ship. Since he went away, the plague came, and my mother died."

Her voice quivered.

"I manage," she went on, "by begging and going to the prisons. There are many in those prisons, and I run errands for them. That lets me earn just enough. When people come to Venice, they don't know where to stay, so I also rent my room. Or try to. Most of the time when people look at me, they turn away. You were different. When I saw you, I hadn't rented my room for three weeks. Or eaten for two days."

I remembered how anxious she'd been to rent the room. "Do you think your father will come back?" I asked.

"I keep asking Saint Antonio to find him. I worry that the Rowers Guild will learn his galley was lost. If they do, they won't let me keep my room. And Aswad wants to visit his family. But he made a promise to my father, his best friend, to look after me. That's the only reason he stays in Venice. He doesn't say that, but I know it. He's poor like me and lives and sleeps in his gondola. If I'm alone and without a place to live, I might be taken up and set to work in some lace factory. Or placed in a convent. They do that with orphan children."

"Who are 'they'?"

"'The Most Serene Republic.' Venice."

"It doesn't seem serene."

"Say 'secret.' It's the same. In the morning, first thing, we'll go to printing shops and ask about your book."

"Thank you. I know you want your father back. But is there something else you want?"

"A home," she said, "with my family."

"Me too," I said.

We continued to sit there, not talking. She closed her eyes and fell asleep, head resting in the crook of her arm, all the while clutching the coin.

Though worn-out, I was unable to sleep. I kept thinking how we were in a race — Bianca and me against the

Black Robes — me in a race to find the friar, get his book, and free Mangus. She to stay alive.

I had to protect myself, and now so did Bianca. It was clear that if I didn't, I would never leave Venice. But I needed her to protect me, too.

If two people depended on each other to live, I supposed that meant we had become friends.

"Bianca," I said, though I knew she was sleeping, "I'll help you. Just like you're helping me."

If only I knew how.

CHAPTER 24

I FELT MY ARM SHAKEN.

Bianca was leaning over me. "Get up. We need to go to those printing places."

I looked around. It was morning.

Stiff, cold, and famished, I got up. As usual, Bianca started off, and I had to hurry behind. Passageways were already crowded with people wearing masks.

"When will people stop wearing masks?"

"As soon as carnival ends."

"When's that?'

"In a few days."

As always, our walk meant a winding trail through alleys and over canals. Then, to my surprise, I saw we had reached the entryway that led to Bianca's campo.

I said, "Why are we going to your room?"

"To hide away my prison key. If I lose it, we'll never get to your master. Wait for me here."

"What if it's being watched?"

"I'll be careful."

She darted into the darkness and was gone.

Uneasy, I waited outside by the canal. The leaden sky was full of swirling gray clouds. A blustery wind made it colder than the day before. Thinking how close I had come to drowning — twice during the previous day — my stomach stirred. I was also on alert for our enemies, which was hard with so many people passing by. To my relief, I didn't see anyone to worry me.

Bianca returned. "The campo was empty. No one saw me," she said. "The key is safe."

We went to four printing shops. None were helpful. The fifth proved otherwise. It came after our usual twisty way when Bianca led us to a building at the head of a lane that ended in a small campo. Facing it was a wide building with an open door. We looked into a large room with three printing machines, which I recognized because I had seen one in Pergamontio. Men were clustered about them, working. Others were setting type. Some were inking. The smell of that ink — lamp black and linseed oil — was strong. Sheets of printed pages hung drying from rafters.

As we stood there, a thin-faced man with cheerful eyes approached us. Dark hair almost reached his shoulders.

"Signor Paganini at your service," he said with a courteous bow. "What can I do for you?"

"Signore," said Bianca, "we want to know if a book was printed here."

As if pleased to be asked, he smiled. "Does it have a title?"

"I'm not sure," I said. "I just know the man who wrote it. Brother Luca Pacioli."

His smile went, replaced by a frown. "Brother Luca. Yes, I'm his printer. His most recent book is an encyclopedia about mathematics, and we shall publish it. Why are you interested?"

"My master needs it."

"*Needs* it?"

"Yes, Signore."

"And your master is?"

"Mangus of Pergamontio."

"Pergamontio." His frown deepened.

"Please, Signore," said Bianca. "Did someone else come here?"

"A man — I don't know his name — came yesterday. Not pleasant. Full of bluster and demands. A Black Robe."

"Did you give him the book?" I asked.

"I did not. We have printed only one copy of Brother Luca's book. A practice printing. I told that man I would talk to the friar about his request. He said he would return. Not long after, Brother Luca came to work on his book, and of course, I told him what had happened."

"What did he do?"

"He asked for that one copy and rushed away with it. He said he needed to make corrections. Then that Black Robe returned."

"What did you tell him?"

"That Brother Luca took his book and went somewhere."

"Where?" asked Bianca.

"I assure you, I have no idea. Do you wish to leave your name for the friar, for when he comes back?"

"I think not, Signore."

Bianca and I walked off. I didn't need to think long about what we had heard. I said, "We have to find where Brother Luca has gone, fast."

Bianca said, "You said Pacioli is a Franciscan monk. The biggest Franciscan church is Santa Maria Gloriosa dei Frari. Someone there may know where he went. It's not far."

"You always say nothing is far," I said.

"Galley rowers say, 'When you know where you are going, the distance is never far.'"

We set off, and after moving through a thin lane, Bianca made a sharp turn, crossed a wide bridge over a canal, and said, "That's the Frari." She pointed to the far side of a wide campo, where a church stood.

It was a huge stone-faced building, topped by three pointy towers. From the rear of the building, a tower rose higher than the church itself.

The entryway was a big wooden door with an arch sculptured over it and columns on either side. A few people — older women — were going in and out. Bianca and I followed them in.

It was a vast church. Twelve gigantic, towering columns arranged in a double row held up the vaulted ceiling with its multiple crisscrossing beams. The air smelled of incense and simmered with soft murmurs, the sound of people whispering prayers. Franciscan friars and nuns in brown robes with white rope belts were moving quietly about the space.

We came in and genuflected but stayed near the two large fonts of holy water by the entryway. At various places along the side aisles, I saw small chapels, in front of which people were kneeling, among them brothers.

Bianca said, "Ask one of the brothers."

I picked one out who was using a taper to light a cluster of candles before an altar. We stood by him, not saying anything. After the brother lit the last candle, he turned about. He was a young man, with a smooth face and rather large eyes. A plain wooden cross hung by a cord from his belt.

"Peace and blessing," he said, lifting a hand in benediction. "May I help you?"

"With permission, Brother," I said. "I'm looking for Brother Luca Pacioli."

The friar smiled. "Many brothers live here. I'm afraid I don't know them all."

"He's a mathematician."

"I still don't know him."

"With permission, Brother, we must speak to him."

"Can you tell me why?"

"He has written a book," said Bianca. "We need to have it."

"Can you read?"

"Yes, Brother," said Bianca. "We both can."

The brother wagged his head toward Bianca. "Is she your sister?"

I glanced at her. She was gazing at the brother. I turned back to the friar. "With permission," I said. "She is."

Bianca shot an angry look at me.

"Maybe Brother Teodore knows the friar of whom you speak. He's the under-abbot in charge of the dormitory. My name is Brother Marco. Please come with me."

He walked down the wide central aisle. Bianca and I followed.

"Why did you say I was your sister?" said Bianca in a hushed voice.

I shrugged.

"I had two sisters."

"Where are they?"

"Dead in the plague." Her voice shook.

"I'm sorry," I said, feeling awful.

After moving down the middle of the church, Brother Marco turned to the right, passing a large choir stall.

"The sacristy," he said, pointing farther along, before going through a door. Inside the small, high room, there were multiple cubbyholes where vestments and robes hung. On the wall was a large painting of the Madonna holding the Child.

Brother Marco put his hand on another doorknob, then paused. "The chapter house." To Bianca, he said, "I'm sorry. Women are not allowed."

Bianca screwed up her face in annoyance and pointed to the painting. "She's here."

"Well, yes, but —" began the brother, but Bianca cut him off by saying, "I'll wait."

Brother Marco opened the door and bade me go through. I looked to Bianca apologetically, but all the same, I followed the brother. The door closed behind me.

CHAPTER 25

I WAS AT THE HEAD OF A LARGE ROOM. IN FRONT OF ME was a high writing table, behind which sat an older brother in his brown robes.

The friar behind the desk looked up.

"Yes, Brother Marco? What can I do for you?" He did not bother to look at me.

Brother Marco made a slight bow. "Brother Teodore, this boy is looking for Brother Luca Pacioli. Do you know where he might be?"

"Brother Luca," he echoed as if tasting the name and not liking it in his mouth. "Why do you ask?"

Brother Marco looked to me for an answer.

"With permission, Brother," I said. "He has written something I need."

"Most odd," said the brother from behind his desk. He rubbed the top of his head. "This morning, I had the same request. What makes our Brother Luca so popular?"

"I can't say," I said, unwilling to tell the truth. "Who was the man?" I asked.

"A Black Robe," said Brother Teodore. "In any case, just yesterday Brother Luca requested permission to go to the monastery on the island of San Francesco to seek quiet to work on a book. That island, you should know, was where our own Saint Francis once lived. You can seek Brother Luca there."

"With permission, Brother," I said, "did you tell that to the Black Robe?"

"Why should I tell you one thing and him another?" he said with a scowl.

In haste, I made my thanks along with a bow and was led out of the hall by Brother Marco. Bianca was waiting. After thanking the brother, Bianca and I walked from the church. "Did you learn anything?" she asked once we were outside.

"We may already be too late."

"What do you mean?"

I repeated what the under-abbot had said, about Brother Luca's whereabouts. And that a Black Robe had already come seeking him. "Do you know," I asked Bianca, "where San Francesco island is?"

"There are so many islands," she said with one of her shrugs. "But Aswad will know."

"Would he take us there?"

"We can ask."

I looked up at the sky. The clouds had become thicker, darker. "We need to get to that monastery," I said. "But I should bring food to my master first."

"What money do you have?"

I held out my remaining coins.

Bianca looked and made a face. "You'll need to spend it all."

I asked, "Do you have your prison key?"

"The prison hallway isn't locked during the day. You can hand food in through the bars. Why," she demanded, changing the subject, "did you call me your sister?"

I shrugged. "It was easier."

Silent, she stood in place. Then, looking straight at me, her face stern, she said, "When my mother and sisters died in the plague, I was left alone. It was as if I were left in the bottom of a well. It was a terrible time."

"Forgive me," I said, feeling inept.

"Maybe," she said, turning away.

"I hope," I offered, "your father will return."

"He has to," she said. "I have nothing now. If he's gone, I'll have less than nothing." As if to end the conversation there, she headed off in a new direction, saying, "The prisons are this way." I stayed close and said no more.

By the time we reached San Marco's, dark clouds had dropped lower. It had become windier. From a distance, I heard a rumble of thunder. People were scurrying to avoid the coming storm. I took the rest of my money to one of the stalls and bought bread. I broke off a piece, gave it to Bianca, then ate some myself. The rest I saved for Mangus.

We went straight to the Doges' Palazzo, and to the same stairway we had used the night before.

We moved on to the steps. Different soldiers stood on guard. Nonetheless, they greeted Bianca by name.

"Food for criminals?" one asked with a grin.

"Criminals need to eat," she answered without a smile.

"Until they don't," said the other, and drew a hand across his neck and made a grimace. Laughing, he waved us through.

The exchange made me nervous.

Bianca led us up the flight of steps into the palazzo. As we walked along, Bianca said, "Against the wall!" I saw why. Coming toward us was a group of men, some in red robes, and others in black. Amid them was an older man with a full white beard, golden robes, and a pointy cap on his head.

Astonished and frightened by the magnificence, I pressed back against the wall.

"Agostino Barbarigo," Bianca whispered. "The doge. The leader of Venice."

The splendid group, full of importance, swept past, paying us no attention whatsoever.

We went on.

That man who had been on guard, Federico, was not at the entrance to the prisons, which meant we were able to go right into the prison hall. Within the dreary cells, prisoners were sprawled about, looking cold and miserable. Two of them noticed Bianca and cried out.

"Bianca, any messages for me?"

"Bianca, did you bring food for me?"

"No, nothing," she answered. "Not today. If they bring me something, I'll get it to you." To another, she said, "You owe me money."

We reached the cell in which, the night before, we had found Mangus. When I looked in, the old man seemed to be asleep on the wooden bed.

"Master," I cried. "It's me, Fabrizio."

He didn't stir.

"Master," I called again.

The sleeping man rolled over. It wasn't Mangus.

CHAPTER 26

TAKEN ABACK, I CALLED, "WITH PERMISSION, SIGNORE. Who are you?"

"Roberto Vartola. And you? And why are you asking?"

"My master, Mangus of Pergamontio, was in this cell last night. Where is he?"

"The old man?"

"Yes."

"They took him away."

"Who did? Why?"

"I've no idea. Black Robes. They never reveal why they do things. When they put me in here, they led him out. If he's brought back, I'll tell him you were here. Are you his son?"

"With permission, just his servant."

"I'll let him know," said the man, and he rolled over on the bed, his back to us.

Upset, I stepped away from the iron bars. "What can I do?" I asked Bianca.

"Nothing," she said. "It doesn't mean your master has

been harmed. They may be just questioning him. Or he may have been shifted to another cell. We'll come back later and see if he was returned."

As we walked back along the stone corridor, we passed the other cells. I peered into each one. I saw nothing of Mangus.

We left the Doges' Palazzo. "Bianca," I blurted out. "We need to find my master."

"We better go to that island monastery."

"Why?"

"To find the friar. It's what your master wanted. I can go into the prisons, but there's no way we can search the palazzo."

Half of me wanted to stay near where Mangus was. The other half wanted me to hurry away in search of Brother Luca.

"Doing something is twice as good as doing nothing," Bianca urged.

I knew she was right.

Not talking, she guided us back to the edge of the canal where we had met Aswad the night before. By the time we reached it, we had eaten the bread, and the sky had become darker. A thick haze blew about us. Bianca put her fingers in her mouth and sent out her whistle. There was no response.

Bianca looked up. "It's going to be a strong storm," she said.

"Can we still go?"

"Aswad will decide."

"Where is he?" I said, distressed that we were taking so long to get going.

"He must be working, taking someone somewhere," she said. "We'll have to wait."

We remained by the canal's edge, her bare feet dangling over the brick berm. As we continued to sit, neither of us spoke. As we sat there, Bianca practiced the trick with the coin. I could see she was getting better.

"You're really good," I told her.

She focused on the coin, practicing even more.

A chilly blanket of gray mist surrounded us. It was hard to see. Bianca shivered and stopped practicing with the coin. Her face became sad.

"What is it?" I asked.

"I don't think my father will come back," she said, her voice shaky.

"Why?"

"It's been too long."

"What might have happened?"

There was a flash of light, then a rolling rumble of thunder overhead. Bianca looked up. "Storms take ships down. Or he might have been captured by someone." She paused a moment. "Sold into slavery."

"Is that possible?"

Unable to speak, merely nodding, she continued to turn the coin in her hand over and over.

I said, "What can you do?"

It took some moments for her to find her voice. "I can pray he returns. Galley fleets can be gone for a long time. Maybe they're seeking nutmeg, which is far away but worth a fortune. Maybe he'll come back rich." She sat without talking, staring I knew not where. Then she put her fingers in her mouth and made another loud whistle. This time it was returned.

"Good," she said. "Aswad's coming." She seemed relieved not to talk anymore.

Aswad and his gondola came into view. "Bianca," he called. "What's happened now?"

"The island of San Francesco. Do you know where it is?"

"A monastery with a few brothers. Off Burano. About five and a half miles away."

Bianca gestured to me. "He wants to go."

"Why?"

"He needs to find a friar."

"And you?"

"Me too."

"It's a long way," said a reluctant Aswad. "Two hours, at least." A rumble of thunder made Aswad look into the sky. "And" he added, "a squall is coming. If we had a bigger boat —"

I said, "My master's life is in danger."

"Aswad, please," Bianca added. "We have to go now. I've no one else to turn to."

I felt like hugging her.

Aswad sighed and said, "I know you pray for your father's return. So do I. All right. Get in."

"Many thanks," said Bianca, somewhat abashed.

We climbed into the gondola. Aswad took his regular post, standing in the stern. Bianca was up at the bow, kneeling. I was in the middle, clutching my knees.

As soon as we were settled, Aswad pulled up his long oar, set it on its post, and began to row. The gondola moved forward, the oar splashing while making its bumping noise against its post.

"Do you want my help?" Bianca called back to the gondolier.

"Soon."

We moved along the canal, making some sharp turns into other canals, all of them hemmed in by hazy, ghost-like buildings on either side. The canal's water was cold and choppy. When I looked up, all I saw were dark tumbling clouds.

With an unexpected swing, Aswad moved the gondola into open water. No more embankments or buildings, nothing but windblown, cold wet spray.

"Where are we?" I called out to Bianca.

"In the lagoon. The water surrounding the city."

Remembering that Aswad had said it would take two hours to reach San Francesco island, I told myself to be patient. Even as I did, there was a close flash of lightning, then booming thunder. Startled, I shivered. The gondola seemed frailer and more unprotected than anything I had ever been in before.

CHAPTER 27

As we moved on, the mist thickened into a fog, swirling about us and making it hard to see far. A boat appeared as if oozing out of a low cloud. I saw enough of it to realize it was a topo, its single, triangular yellow sail billowing. Bigger than our gondola, her sail bore a large painted black cross. It didn't take long before she was swallowed up by the fog. It made me wish we could move as fast.

Are our enemies on that boat heading to where we are going? If so, they would get there first.

Knowing there was nothing I could do about it, I kept my mouth shut.

Instead, I tried to think about what I would say to Brother Luca if I found him at the monastery. What, I wondered, did he look like? Would he talk to me, or even share his book with its secrets? Would I have to steal it? Mangus had suggested the friar might have power or money enough to free him from prison. What if he didn't? I clutched my knees tighter and stared into the mist. That was the only answer I had.

As we moved farther from the city, the wind blustered. Lightning and thunder became more frequent. The lagoon water became choppy. White-crested waves began to smack against our gondola, making it sway and bounce. I held on, my jaw aching from constant nervous clamping.

"Bianca," called Aswad, "I could use your help now. There's a paddle up in the bow."

Kneeling, she picked up a small oar, dipped it into the water, and began to row.

"That'll help keep us steady," Aswad said.

I glanced around. I saw nothing ahead and nothing behind. No one else seemed to be in the lagoon but us. I thought again about that topo. Where was it heading? I marveled how Aswad knew where to go. How he controlled his gondola.

A crack of lightning and its flash of light seemed to explode right over our heads, making me duck. That was followed by booming thunder. Rain poured down, then eased somewhat, which allowed me to see a small island.

"Is that where we are going?" I called out, pointing.

Aswad called back. "That's Murano. Where they make glass. We need to go farther. Near Burano."

As he spoke, there was another crash of lightning. It sounded like a shooting cannon. A rattling of more thunder, followed by lashing sheets of squally rain, made it much harder to see.

Water was streaming down Aswad's face, but he kept his place and continued his steady rowing, his oar groaning. He was leaning into his strokes so that his whole body moved, head jutted forward as he tried to see through the wash of driving rain.

A drenched Bianca, before me, continued her paddling, too.

I, of course, was doing nothing — other than getting soaked — trying to hide the fact that the harsh weather and roiling lagoon water frightened me and made me nauseous. I also remembered something I had read: A storm was an omen. It meant that someone was going to be hanged. Or, I thought, drowned. I held on to our boat tighter.

Rain was pooling at the bottom of our boat. Looking about, I saw a small wooden bowl. I snatched it up and began to scoop up water and throw it overboard. I didn't accomplish very much, but it was better than doing nothing.

Though the rain ceased, a swirling fog wrapped around us. Within moments, the rain resumed, but it was thin so at least I could see farther over the lagoon.

We approached the island of Murano, upon which I saw quite a few buildings, none more than two stories high. But Aswad turned his gondola to the right and headed toward a cluster of smaller islands. As we drew near, I saw that they were covered with grasses and a few low structures. We passed into a channel that took us through the islands, where there was less turbulent water.

All too soon we came out from those islands and onto another expanse of water, which was bumpy again. Lightning crackled, followed, as always, by thunder. All the while, Bianca and Aswad kept rowing.

The storm grew wilder. Our slim gondola pitched up and down like a pump handle. Then the rain eased somewhat. Our boat settled. Soaking wet, bone chilled, we went on.

"San Francesco island ahead," Aswad called out.

Beginning to see a little better, I made out a cluster of small islands before us. My tension eased. With any luck, Brother Luca and his book were in reach.

We entered a calm canal that allowed us to go deep into an island's interior. All was silent, save for the slow, soft *swish* of Aswad's long oar and the soft *pit-patter* of rain. As far as I could see, the island seemed to have nothing but cypress trees and gardens. There were no other boats around, which I found unsettling.

The rain continued along with a clotted vapor, which hovered over us. The cloud — if that's what it was — clung to the ground, making everything blurry.

The canal ended at a stone landing.

"Here you are," Aswad announced as he maneuvered us to a soft stop.

Bianca climbed out first. Finding some old rope, she fixed our gondola to a wooden post. On shaky legs, I followed, unable to stand very well.

"I'm coming with you," said Aswad. "I need some dryness."

"Come on," Bianca replied.

Seeing a wide gravel path, I said, "That way."

As the rain continued, the three of us walked side by side down the path. The only sound was the crunch of our feet on the gravel.

I began to see a cluster of low brick buildings of two levels. I also saw a tower whose top was lost in the mist. I assumed I was seeing the monastery. On the building closest to us, I noticed a wide-open entryway flanked by two large windows.

But we had yet to see anyone. It was as if the island had been abandoned. Then, from somewhere, a bird sent out a single sharp whistle. It sounded like a warning.

We stopped. When nothing happened, we kept on, but slower.

We went through the entryway into a cloister. The familiar well stood in the middle. The area had uneven gray stones and slender weathered columns. Puddles were everywhere. The quiet was deep. We still saw no people. It was hard to think of this island as a part of raucous Venice.

"Maybe no one is here," said Bianca.

"Wait," said Aswad. "I smell wood burning."

On the far side of the cloister, I saw another doorway. By its side hung a rusty bell to which was attached a knotted rope. Looking through the doorway, I saw a long hallway, as deserted as everything else. A single candle with a small quivering flame was stuck into the stone wall.

Aswad reached up and pulled the bell rope three times. The clang had a low tone — like a death knell.

We waited. The rain intensified.

CHAPTER 28

IT SEEMED LIKE A LONG TIME BEFORE WE SAW A MAN coming toward us from the far end of the hallway. His brown robe and white belt told me he was a Franciscan.

"God be with you," the brother said as he approached. Long faced, with sad eyes, he was ill-shaved and bore a troubled look.

"Brother Angelo at your service," he said in a soft voice. "You picked a harsh day to visit. But you are welcome." He made a slight bow, hands enfolded in his robe sleeves.

"With permission," I began. "We —"

"You've come through that storm," he interrupted. "You're wet and cold. Come sit by the fire. Soup and bread will do you good. Then you can tell me why you're here."

Without waiting for our response, the brother turned and headed back down the hallway. We followed.

"There are six of us living here," he said as he walked on. "We're isolated, so few come. Yet today we already had another visit. Most unpleasant. My brothers felt so threatened they've gone into hiding. You must forgive them."

Bianca and I exchanged looks.

"Where are you from?" the brother asked.

Bianca said, "Venice."

Brother Angelo halted and turned to face us. He looked distressed. "Earlier, two men came here — Black Robes. They insisted on speaking to one of our brothers."

"What brother did they ask for?"

"Brother Luca."

"Is Brother Luca here?" said Bianca.

"Why are you asking?"

I said, "With permission, we need to see him."

"What do you want of him?"

"He's written a book," I explained.

"That's what those men said. They *demanded* Brother Luca. Indeed, they threatened. As I told you, they were so angry that my brethren retreated for prayer. We are not used to violence. I need to know, are you with those men?"

"Not at all," said Bianca.

I said, "Did they speak to Brother Luca?"

"Part of my vows is that I must always speak the truth no matter how hard," said Brother Angelo. "It's for God to decide the consequences. Now come along. Have some food and warmth. Then I will answer your questions." With that, he turned about and continued along the hallway.

The brother led us into a small room where there was a hearth with a fire burning and over the low flames a warming pot. There was also a long table with benches. On the table were wooden bowls and spoons. A simple wooden cross hung on the wall.

"Please, sit," said the brother.

Though I wanted to hear more about Brother Luca, I was glad to rest on something solid. The warmth of the room was equally welcome, the smell of food alluring.

Brother Angelo served us in silence, filling the bowls with something thick that smelled like meat broth. He provided large slices of dark bread. After reciting a short prayer of blessing, he said, "Please, eat."

After we had eaten some, the brother said, "Now, tell me, what brings you in search of Brother Luca?"

Both Aswad and Bianca looked at me.

"He has written a book."

"Many have written books. Why is this one so important?"

"It reveals a way of making money," I said.

Brother Angelo put his hands together and said, "'He who loves money will not be satisfied with money.' Ecclesiastes 5:10."

I said, "My master is in prison — in Venice — accused by the same men who visited you."

"Of what has he been accused?"

Afraid to say *magic*, I only said, "I don't think it's anything he's done. And my master believes Brother Luca is the only person who can free him. We need to find him."

"What is your name?"

"Fabrizio, Brother."

"You should know, one of the men who came here asked about you, by name. He wanted to know if you had been here."

"Please," said Bianca. "Is Brother Luca here?"

"Those men were so hostile that we were forced to keep Brother Luca hidden."

"So he was here," I cried.

"He was."

"*Was?*" asked Bianca.

"He fled."

"Where?" I said.

Brother Angelo looked distressed.

"With permission, Brother," I said. "By all that's sacred, we wish him no harm. We just need to speak to him."

The brother remained silent for a while longer, as if struggling with some inner thought. Then he said, "Brother Luca claimed he knew of a safe and secret hiding place."

"Where?" I asked.

"He didn't say. But I can guess."

"Where?"

"The cathedral on Torcello."

I turned to Aswad.

"Farther north," he said. "An island past Murano. People say it's the oldest part of Venice."

I asked, "How far is it?"

"Maybe another mile," said Aswad.

"Do those men who threatened you know about

Torcello?" asked Bianca. "And that Brother Luca might be there?"

"I said nothing. But they, too, might have guessed. There are not that many safe places one might hide out here."

I shifted around first to look at Aswad. "Can we go there?" I asked.

Aswad looked to Bianca. "I'm tired," he said forthrightly to her. "If you wish, I can take you there. It's not that far. But when we get there, I'll need to rest. It's a long way back."

"Please," she said to him.

"Very well," said Aswad.

I stood up. "With permission, Brother, we have to go."

"Peace," I heard Brother Angelo call as we rushed away. I hoped we would find some.

CHAPTER 29

WE WERE BETTER FED WHEN WE REACHED THE gondola and somewhat dryer, but the rain was still falling. As soon as Bianca untied Aswad's boat, we got in. He, as always, stood on the stern. I was in the middle. With Bianca settled in the bow, Aswad started to row. It took only moments for us to get out of the island's small canal and move once again over the lagoon.

Gazing through the grayness, I saw a few islands, the largest of which held a cluster of low buildings.

"Is that Torcello?"

"Burano," said Bianca. "Where they make lace. If my father doesn't come back, that's where they might send me." Then she added, "It would be like a prison."

With steady strokes, Aswad rowed on. The rain continued with more lightning and thunder. We were soaked anew. It also grew colder.

As we skirted the island of Burano, I could make out what looked to be a village. Any number of boats was tied up along its wharves. Among them, I noticed a topo with a yellow sail, like the one I had seen before. The sail was slack, which meant the boat was not moving. I thought I saw people in it. My immediate fear was that I was seeing our enemies. Uncertain, not wanting to put pressure on Aswad, I kept my suspicions to myself.

Aswad took us into a wide river. I kept looking back. That topo was nowhere in sight, but the rain made it hard to see, so I wasn't sure.

We moved on. The land to either side of us was low, with a fair number of trees and a few buildings. Ahead, through the curtain of rain, I began to make out a tall, square tower. I hoped it was Torcello's cathedral.

We made a sharp turn to the right and entered a narrow canal. As we did, the rain intensified, beating down harder. I could no longer see the cathedral.

The canal came to an end at a stone landing. As soon as Aswad put down his oar, Bianca jumped out and tied us to a post.

Drenched, I got out and looked around. An open area lay before us. Being closer, I could saw more of the cathedral. It was a heavy-looking gray building, squat, and square in shape. I saw no one and heard nothing but the constant wash of the pelting rain. Everything seemed desolate.

After tying our gondola to the landing place, we walked along a brick path, trying to avoid deep puddles. Bianca, with her bare feet, didn't seem to care. I kept looking for people. Not a soul. After a while, we came upon a tavern with a light inside. We went to the door and peered in, seeing only empty tables. No people.

We stepped out of the rain. "Where is everyone?" I asked.

"They don't expect people during a storm," suggested Bianca.

"Are you going to wait for the storm to pass?" asked Aswad.

"I think we should go on to the cathedral," I said.

"I agree," said Bianca.

"You two go along and look for your brother," said Aswad. "I can stay here. I need to rest and dry out a bit."

He went to a chair and sat down, the rainwater pooling around his feet. He looked exhausted. "Be careful," he called. His eyes were already closing.

"I worry about him," Bianca said, glancing back as we continued along the brick path. "He looks after me well, but it's hard on him. He'd be better off without me to worry about."

As we drew closer to the cathedral, I made out an open porch entryway. Glad to get under cover, we stood in place dripping wet. We looked about but still saw no one.

"What if he's not here?" I said.

"Only one way to find out," said Bianca.

As we stepped into the cathedral, my soggy clothing made me shiver.

It may have been a cathedral, but it was nowhere near as large as the Frari. But it looked and felt ancient, altogether melancholy with many shadowy corners in its dim interior. The only light came from a cluster of small, sputtering candles on the altar near the front of the church, which made me think of a bed of little flowers.

Along each side of the nave stood a row of tall, pale green stone columns. In front of the chancel, a pulpit. On the uneven floor lay small, well-worn multicolored stones. High above us, the pelting rain beat upon the roof like the constant roll of a drum. The echoing sound enhanced the feeling that the building was deserted.

That said, the walls were populated with images of hundreds of people. An enormous and grave Jesus, round-eyed saints with golden halos, austere apostles, bulky bishops, flocks of winged angels. There were also white-robed people rising to the light of heaven, as well as naked people tumbling into demon fire, where skulls lay with eye sockets filled with crawly snakes. All the images had been composed with tiny bits of colored stone or glass — mosaic — which, reflecting the soft fluttering candlelight, made them seem to tremble with life.

But it was to the front of the church, the curved apse, that my eyes were drawn. There, behind a decorated partition wall, was an immense image of Mary. Standing perfectly still in her hooded black gown, she gazed out mournfully. A single large tear was depicted falling from one eye. But it felt as if both of her dark eyes were looking at me, accusing me of failing her. As Bianca and I meandered about separately, Mary's eyes seemed to follow me no matter where I went.

I saw no sign of Brother Luca.

"Is anyone here?" I called. No reply. I called again. No answer, just the rain beating down above.

Bianca and I met at the crossing. She nodded toward the image of Mary. "She keeps watching me."

"Me too. But I don't think anyone living is here."

Bianca said, "We need to get back to Aswad."

Disappointed not to have found Pacioli, we went back to the entryway and stared out at the falling rain. It was sluicing down, pounding with a steady thrum, making ever-bigger puddles to either side of the brick walk. Feeling dejected, and not sure what else to do, we continued to stand there, waiting for the rain to slacken. I felt we had failed. Failed to find Brother Luca. Failed Mangus.

It was as we stood there, looking outward, caught up in our thoughts, that a figure stepped out through the curtain of rain. I recognized him instantly. His spiky red beard, thin lips, and dagger in hand revealed him as the assassin he was: the royal tax collector of Pergamontio, Lorenzo Rozetti.

CHAPTER 30

THE MOMENT I SAW HIM, I HAD NO DOUBT Pergamontio's royal tax collector was there to collect me.

I also knew the person who was by his side: Signor Cardano.

Short, bulked with muscle, he had a sword in his hand.

"It's them," I said under my breath, scarcely believing my eyes. "The tall one has chased me all the way from my home. The short one is the Black Robe I met on the galley coming here."

As one, Bianca and I spun back into the cathedral in search of a hiding place. In all that open building, the only spot to hide was behind the altar right below the image of Mary. We crouched down.

"Do you think they saw us?" I said, keeping my voice low.

"Don't know."

After a few moments, I heard Rozetti's shrill voice: "He said they were in here." The two men had entered the cathedral.

Into my ear, Bianca said, "They must have found Aswad and made him say where we were."

"I hope they didn't hurt him," I said.

Bianca pulled hard at my arm and pointed to a large dark hole in the stone floor. Steep stone steps led down into darkness.

"Where does it go?" I whispered.

"The crypt, probably," she said.

I looked questioningly at her.

She said, "Where important dead people are buried."

"Could it be a way out?" I asked.

We heard Rozetti and Cardano moving about the cathedral. The next moment, there was a shout: "Fabrizio, you've failed. We've found you. It's over."

"Come on," urged Bianca, and she moved toward the crypt steps.

I stole a quick look over the altar into the church's main aisle. I saw both men, wandering about the cathedral's far end, weapons in hand.

Taking a chance, I jumped up, reached out, and grabbed one of the altar's small burning candles.

Thankfully, I wasn't seen. I went to the edge of the crypt steps and held the candle over the hole. I saw no bottom.

Whispering, Bianca said, "Maybe it'll get us back to Aswad."

I hesitated, only to hear Rozetti's loud voice — "Fabrizio, I know you're here."

"No other place to go," Bianca said into my ear.

Keeping the candle before me, I started down the extremely steep steps. Bianca was right behind.

My bubble of candlelight only showed that we were moving into deeper darkness. The sharp downward tilt of the steps forced me to take one careful step at a time even as I pressed the palm of my free hand against the cold stone wall to keep from falling. Though I wished we had more light, we continued moving down, the only sound being our soft and wary footfalls.

I had no idea how far we needed to go save that the farther we went, the blacker and chillier it became. It was as if, like those images on the cathedral walls, we were descending into a cold hell. I half expected demons, and those snake-stuffed skulls, to be waiting at the bottom — if we ever reached it. When I paused and looked back at the square of faint light above, it seemed very far away. And with every further step down, that square seemed to become smaller.

It felt forever before we came off the lowest step onto a hard stone floor. When we did, it was into about two inches of water.

I held up my candle and gazed about. We were in a cave-like place, with a pale, cross-vaulted brick ceiling. A corridor led from where we stood into more darkness. The still air smelled of mold and rot. I could hear nothing but my own and Bianca's breathing.

Huge white stone boxes with stone slab covers stood around us, arranged like spokes on a wagon wheel. Carved into the side of each box were large Eastern crosses, Latin writing, and Roman numerals.

"Coffins," Bianca whispered.

"Why are they so big?"

"They put smaller coffins into them."

"Whose?"

"Bishops, I guess."

My candle flame allowed me to see and hear water trickling in from the dark passageway where we stood. Whether it was coming from the rain or the lagoon, I had no idea.

I peered back up the steps from which we had just descended. The top opening was nothing but a faint gray square. But I could hear Rozetti's and Cardano's footsteps as they wandered about.

Into my ear, Bianca said: "I'm worried about Aswad."

"Me too."

As we continued to stand there, my eyes adjusted to the dark. Staring down the hallway, instead of total blackness, I began to make out a faint glow at its far end.

Pointing, I said, "A way out, maybe. We might be able to avoid going back through the cathedral."

I heard more movement above. It seemed as if Rozetti was coming closer to the steps behind the altar.

Bianca must have sensed that, too. She pulled at me. "Let's go," she said.

Staying close together, we started along the dark corridor. I continued to hold out the small candle, which provided a thin and quivering yellow light. As we sloshed through the cold water, we made a soft splattering. It did occur to me that the passageway might end or become impassable, which meant we'd be trapped. Not knowing what else to do, I said nothing.

We walked forward. The farther we went, the deeper the water became. It gave me the sensation that the ceiling was getting lower. I could only hope it wasn't so.

We came upon a large alcove built into the wall's left side. The crumbling brick walls bore patches of green slime. Its floor being somewhat higher than where we stood, I could see that it held no water. There were also more of those large stone coffins. A few of them had no slab tops. That's to say, they were open.

"Wait," I said.

Thinking the alcove might serve — if necessary — as a hiding place, I climbed up and, using the candle, peered into one of the stone boxes. What I saw appeared to be not a coffin but a body wrapped in frayed cloth. I peered into another coffin. That one was empty.

"If they come down after us, we could hide in here," I said.

"Be better," said Bianca, "if we could get out through the other end of this place. Come on."

I started to come out of the alcove only to slip on some of that slime. Impulsively — to keep from falling — I reached for a wall. That caused my candle to fall from my hand and drop into the water. With a tiny *sisss*, its flame went out. It became much darker.

"Fool," I muttered.

For a moment, we stood still, not sure what to do. But that dim light was still visible from farther along the corridor. Now that it was darker, it seemed brighter.

Bianca pulled at me. "We need to go faster," she said.

She took the lead as we moved toward that glimmering. The light seemed to be coming from another alcove, this time on the right. As we drew closer, it grew brighter and fluttered, suggesting a burning candle.

"Someone," I muttered.

Trying to be as quiet as possible, we waded forward.

I began to hear a slight scratching sound.

"Wait," I said, listening hard.

Bianca cocked her head. "Rats," she said.

Belatedly, I realized it was like what I'd often heard coming from Mangus's study at night: someone writing, pen to paper.

"I don't think so."

We edged forward and peered around a corner. It was another alcove, big enough to be a room. Like the other, it was somewhat higher than the corridor, so there was no water on its floor. There was also a tall wooden desk, upon which a burning candle had been placed, the wax pooling at its base.

Before the desk stood a man.

He was dressed in the hooded brown robe of a Franciscan friar, with the white knotted rope around his waist. He wore leather sandals on his feet. He was leaning over a thick pile of paper, reading and marking it with a quill pen. On the ground lay a leather sack. He was concentrating so hard he must not have heard us come but continued working even as we stood there staring.

After a few moments, I said, "With permission, are you Brother Luca Pacioli?"

CHAPTER 31

THE MAN SPUN ABOUT TO LOOK AT US. THERE WAS nothing hostile in his ruddy, candlelit gaze, just surprise. His face was round, pale, with thin lips and small eyes. His nose was large, and his dark hair was tonsured. I guessed him to be about fifty years of age.

He continued to stare at us, but as he realized we were two cold, wet young people peering up at him out of the dark, the expression on his face shifted to amusement. We must have looked like sodden rabbits.

"Why, yes," he replied, "I'm Brother Luca. Who are you?"

"Bianca."

"Fabrizio."

"And *why* are you here?"

Bianca said, "Brother, there are two armed men up there" — she pointed back toward the cathedral — "who want to steal your book."

"With permission," I added, "the one with the secret method of accounting."

"Ah, yes," said Pacioli. "My brothers on San Francesco

isle warned me about them. Not that I have any idea why they should pursue me. I wouldn't think a book about mathematics mattered so much. Are they close?"

"Yes, Brother," said Bianca. "In the cathedral."

"Who are they?"

"One of them," I said, "is the royal tax collector of Pergamontio. The other is a Black Robe from Venice."

"How do you know about them?"

"They're after us, too," said Bianca.

"Why?"

Feeling my face become hot, I said, "I must confess, Brother, I wanted to steal your book, too. They were trying to get to you before we did."

"Are you still trying to steal the book?"

"With permission, not anymore."

To my relief, he smiled. "But you are here nonetheless," he said.

"We need you to help his master," said Bianca.

"How?"

"He's in prison," I said. "Since you're so famous, you might find a way to free him."

"Extraordinary," said Brother Luca, who continued to gaze upon us with amusement. "Where do you come from?"

"I am from Venice. He's from Pergamontio."

"Are you brother and sister?" he asked.

There was quiet for a moment before Bianca replied. This time, to my surprise, she said, "Yes."

"How did you get to Torcello?"

"My godfather, Aswad, is a gondolier. He brought us."

"With permission, Brother," I urged. "We truly need to go. Those men are coming after you and us. They're dangerous. They might be here any moment. Can we get out this way?" I said, pointing down the corridor.

The friar shook his head. "Alas, it's flooded."

"What about your magic, Brother? Might that be useful?"

He laughed. "Magic? Why should you ask that?"

"Aren't you a magician?"

"To be sure, I use tricks to prove there is no magic. But this doesn't seem to be the time to talk about that," he said. "If what you say is true — about those assassins — we need to find a way to save ourselves."

"And my godfather," said Bianca.

"Is he still here?"

"Above. In a tavern."

As if from a great distance, I was hearing voices from the cathedral. "I think they're coming," I said with urgency. I pointed. "Brother, back there, in an alcove, there's an empty coffin. I think it's big enough to hide us."

"Excellent idea," said Brother Luca. With that, he snatched up the leather sack and stuffed all his papers into it, along with his flint box. Once he did that, he handed his lit candle to me, then stepped down out of the alcove into the water. With me going first, holding the candle before me, we hurried back along the corridor. It took only moments to reach the recess.

I held up the candle. "That's the one," I said, indicating the empty coffin.

The friar took back his candle, climbed into the niche, and peered into the stone box. "Good. It should be big enough."

He gave his candle back to me and then handed Bianca his sack to hold. Moving swiftly, he picked her up and lowered her into the stone box. He did the same to me. Then he pulled himself up to the coffin's edge, swung his legs around, and dropped himself down.

We were now — the three of us — sitting in the huge stone box. Bianca and I sat at opposite ends, with Brother Luca in the middle, his satchel on his lap.

The coffin was cold, hard, and cramped. Our toes kept bumping. Water from our feet and clothing pooled under us, adding to our discomfort. Besides, knowing its purpose made me uneasy. What if a lid was put on it?

"I hadn't expected to be in a coffin so soon," Brother Luca whispered. He seemed to find the situation amusing.

"I'm glad I found you alive," I said.

"So am I," said the brother softly. "But best not talk now." He blew out the candle.

The next second, there wasn't so much as a spark of light. I had never experienced such darkness. When I put my hand right before my face, I couldn't see it.

As we continued to sit there, neither moving nor speaking, I began to hear voices coming from the cathedral end of the corridor.

“They might have come down here,” said a voice. Recognizing Rozetti, I held my breath.

“I don’t see anyone,” said another voice. Cardano, I guessed.

A ray of thin light — shaped like the blade of a knife — appeared on the ceiling above our heads. In its glow, I saw Bianca’s eyes. They were big. Brother Luca’s eyes were closed. I wondered if he was praying. I held my breath.

“The passage goes that way,” I heard Cardano say.

“Any idea where it leads?” asked Rozetti.

“No.”

“I’ve paid you good money to guide me about. You’re not doing well.”

We heard the two men splash through the water.

“It’s getting deeper.”

“It must go to the lagoon. Which means it’s blocked. They must not have gone this way.”

“That boy has a way of disappearing,” said Rozetti with a frustration I hadn’t heard from him before. “Went to his master, I suppose.”

“Maybe that old gondolier wasn’t telling the truth.”

"The point is, no one is here," said Cardano.

"This was a waste of time. We'll have to search for the friar — and the boy — back in the city."

"What about the book?"

"If the boy has it," said Rozetti, "he'll have taken it to Mangus. In the prisons."

"I'll speak to the authorities at the palazzo," said Cardano. "I'll have the old man dealt with."

"How?"

"The boy told me his master was a magician. That's crime enough. He'll be executed."

My heart lurched.

"Fine," continued Rozetti, "but the boy might still be hiding up in the cathedral with that book."

"I doubt it, but we'll search some more."

"If we don't find him, we'll have to get back to the city. I assure you, once I lay my hands on that friar, I have ways to make him give me his book. When I do, I'll deal with that boy once and for all."

"I should have drowned him when I had the chance. Next time."

As the sound of their watery steps receded, the silence and complete darkness returned. But the words I had heard made me near frantic. "Please," I said in an urgent whisper, "I must get back to the city. You heard them. They're going to harm my master."

"Better wait a while," said Brother Luca.

Bianca agreed. "They might still be in the cathedral."

I forced myself to sit still.

"Since we have to wait," said Brother Luca, keeping his voice low, "tell me again; you said you came to steal my book. Why would you do that?"

"It's my king — the king of Pergamontio. He wants to stop you from printing that bookkeeping method. He doesn't want people to learn about it."

Brother Luca gave a snort. "What I've written is not a secret," he replied. "The method is used by many merchants in Venice. All I've done is write it down. And I assure you, it's the smallest section of my encyclopedia. Just a few pages."

I hardly knew how to feel. "Then it was foolish to come to Venice," I said.

The friar laughed. "As it's been said: If you do nothing, you can't make mistakes. But if you don't make mistakes, you learn nothing and stay ignorant."

"Then the more mistakes you make," I said, "the smarter you are."

"Indeed," said the brother, "it takes many failures to make one success."

"But, Brother," I said, "one of these men is a Black Robe. You heard: My master is in danger. They intend him harm. They already managed to imprison him in the Doges' Palazzo."

"What do they look like?"

I described them.

"And," added Bianca, "I'm really worried what they might do to my godfather."

"Do you think," Brother Luca asked, "there might be room in his gondola to take me back to Venice?"

"I'm sure there is," said Bianca.

"When people think of priests, they too often think of death. I prefer to think about life. And young people have more life than anyone. You two have saved my life. I owe you mine. When we get back to the city, you have my word, I'll help you. *Ordo mundi*. Do you know the phrase? It's Latin and means 'God has a way of connecting everything.' I've heard it said, true treasure is not what you seek but what you find. You have found me, and I have found you. Ergo, we are connected. Now, I think we've waited long enough. It's time we try to get away from here."

CHAPTER 32

THOUGH WE WERE STILL SITTING IN COMPLETE darkness, I heard Brother Luca begin to move about. "I shall do that rarest of acts," he announced in a voice tinged with glee. "I'm rising out of my coffin. I'm moving out of the alcove. I'm standing in the passageway. Signora Bianca, wave your hands about. I'll find them and pull you free. Do you have my satchel?"

"Yes, Brother."

Though I didn't see them, I heard them shuffling about.

"Bianca, are your feet set down?"

"Yes, Brother. In the water."

"No help for that. Now, Signor Fabrizio, your turn. Lift your hands."

I held them up. Brother Luca found them, grasped them, and while I scrambled, he pulled me until I got clear of the coffin, and then set me down to the corridor floor. I was calf-deep in the corridor's water.

"All good. Bianca, give me your hand," he said. "Now, take Fabrizio's. Done?"

"Yes."

"Excellent. We're in line. Don't let go, or we shall lose one another. I'll go first. Are we ready?"

"Yes, Brother," Bianca and I said at the same time.

"Here we go. No more talk. As Bianca has reminded us, those two men might be waiting to ambush us. Be ready to run."

"Where?" I whispered.

"Any place you can."

Hands linked, no one talking, Brother Luca moved us through the corridor, sloshing softly through the water. Gradually, a gleaming revealed itself ahead. It was not as if I saw anything. Rather it was a growing awareness that walls surrounded us, and a further sense that, dark though it was, we were moving toward the light. We pressed on. I began to see Bianca and the friar's shadow.

At last, it was the brother who announced, "We've reached the steps."

I saw them for myself. They were illuminated by a square of indistinct light that dropped from the cathedral above. As for the ancient coffin holders, I saw them, too, big, pale, white, and silent.

The three of us stood there, not moving, staring up, and listening. There was nothing to hear, no suggestion that our enemies were above.

"They may be waiting for us," Bianca said.

"It's possible," agreed Brother Luca.

"I'll go look," said Bianca.

"Be careful," I said.

"I'll whistle if it's clear," she called over her shoulder.

She moved up the way we had come down, one riser at a time, soon becoming hardly more than a silhouette. I kept my eyes on her. It wasn't long before she was out of sight.

Brother Luca and I stayed at the foot of the steps, straining to watch and listen. The longer we stood there, the more anxious I became. What if Rozetti was at the top, waiting for one of us to emerge? Maybe their silence was a trap. Where was Bianca?

Brother Luca must have guessed what I was thinking because he put a light hand on my shoulder. I peered back at him. In the soft light, he put a finger to his lips. "Patience," he whispered, "is the silent prayer of saints."

We continued to remain in place until I heard a sharp whistle. Bianca's whistle. Whether a warning or a beckoning, I was not certain. All the same, I shook off the friar's hand and started to climb the steps as fast as possible.

I was halfway up when I saw Bianca's face at the top, looking down. She waved us on.

I kept going. Brother Luca followed.

"I didn't see anybody," Bianca announced as we emerged from the steps into the space behind the altar. "They must have left."

Wanting to search for ourselves, the three of us went into the cathedral space and walked about. Most of the altar candles had gone out or dwindled to stubs, so it was darker, and the many images on the walls seemed to have faded. As for our enemies, we saw no sign of them. It made me more fearful.

"They've gone back to the city," I said. "We have to get there."

"Aswad," said Bianca.

We hurried outside, where the rain had stopped, only to be replaced by a dense fog that made it difficult to see for more than a few feet. All the same, Bianca rushed forward, following the brick path, which I was certain was the same we had taken when we first came.

A two-story building emerged, then faded away. A tree did the same. Then a fuzzy golden light — perhaps a lit lamp — appeared. We headed for that. The structure behind the light emerged. It proved to be the tavern into which Aswad had gone.

Bianca burst in. Pacioli and I followed. At first glance, the room appeared empty. Then we saw Aswad. He was sitting in a chair, hands tied with ropes. I saw a red welt on his neck. Bianca went right up and worked to release him. "Are you all right?"

"Fine," said Aswad. "One of them had a dagger," he added. "When I refused to tell them where you were, they tied me up. I heard them say they were going to the cathedral. I told them nothing. Thankfully, they did you no harm. Who is this?" he asked, looking at the friar.

"Brother Luca," said Bianca, stepping aside.

"And the book?"

Brother Luca lifted his leather sack.

"Tell me what happened."

Bianca told Aswad how we went into and then out of the cathedral crypt.

"And those men?"

"We heard them say they were going back to the city."

"To kill my master," I added. "If we're going to save him, we have to get to the Doges' prisons."

"Then we need to go," said Aswad, rising from his chair.

"May I join you?" asked Brother Luca. "I can help with the rowing."

The four of us hurried back out into the fog and made our way to the gondola. While Bianca untied it, Aswad took up his position at the stern of the boat, long oar in his hands. Brother Luca went to the prow and grasped the paddle that Bianca had used. His leather sack, with his book, was by his side.

Bianca and I sat in the middle. I touched the nail in my pocket and once again told myself to be patient. There were no other oars.

The canal banks that slipped by were not very visible in the fog. Regardless, we made quick progress. It wasn't long before Aswad announced, "We're in the lagoon."

Standing in the stern, he, with Brother Luca in the bow, kept up their steady rowing. Bianca sat in the middle of the gondola, arms wrapped around her knees. I sat near her, my clothing wet and cold. We didn't speak, just waited and watched.

Our trip from Venice to Torcello had been storm-tossed and difficult. Now the weather had turned calm and the lagoon was unruffled. But the air was still clotted with mist, so it was hard to see. It caused me to worry about where our enemies were. Had they gone right back to the city? Had they gone to the prisons and Mangus? I tried to put the thoughts out of my mind.

We kept on.

I don't know how long it took, but in lowering dusk, the lights of Venice rose before us, as if lifting out of the sea.

Leaving the lagoon, Aswad took us into the city by way of a canal, along which buildings crowded in on both sides.

I began to see people walking along the canal's embankments.

Aswad maneuvered his gondola up against some stone steps, where the multiple posts poked out of the water. Once he had made his gondola fast, we climbed out and stood on firm land. To my great relief, we were back in Venice.

"Now where will you go?" asked Aswad.

"We have to get my master out of the prison," I said.

"Is he in one of those palazzo cells?"

"We think so."

"Do we have a way in?" asked Brother Luca.

Bianca said, "I have a key."

The friar looked at her with a smile. "Signora, you are full of surprises."

"Fine, but do you have a way to get him *out* of the palazzo?" said Aswad.

"I'm not sure," admitted Bianca.

"It will be dangerous," he said, with a furrow of his brow. I could see the thought added to his exhaustion.

"Perhaps I can help with that," said Brother Luca.

"How?" I asked.

"Give me some time," the brother replied, and held up his satchel. "First, I need to hide my book somewhere. Those men might waylay us, and I mustn't lose my work."

"We're not far from the Frari," said Bianca.

"Perfect," said the brother.

"Won't they be looking for you there?" Aswad asked.

"We'll have to chance it. It's the safest place for my book."

"After that, we'll go to my room," Bianca said. "Get my key."

"And then to the prisons," I added.

"But you must be very careful," said Aswad to Bianca. "I don't want your father to return, only to have me tell him you've vanished."

"I promise," Bianca said to him.

"Signore," I said to the gondolier, "a million, trillion thanks for all you did. I'm sorry they attacked you."

All he said, and it was more to Bianca than to me, was "I'll be about if you need me."

Brother Luca shook Aswad's hands and blessed him.

As for Bianca, she gave Aswad a hug, plus quick kisses

on his cheeks, which were returned. After an exchange of some private words, we three, following her lead, started moving fast.

Night had come, and the twilight haze made everything harder to see. Streets and alleys, as always, were crowded. Masks were everywhere. Carnival was still going on. None of this hindered Bianca. She led us in her usual brisk, maze-threading way. I kept alert for Rozetti and Cardano, sure they would show up somewhere. Then I had the thought: *What if they are wearing masks?* There were so many people who had them: Masks were the perfect disguise.

It wasn't long before we crossed a wide bridge over a canal and stepped onto the campo that lay before the huge Frari. The round colored-glass window over the church door was lit from behind, and the church's big front doors were open. Large lamps had been hung up to either side, perhaps because of the fog. We saw people going into the church for Mass. As we stood there, bells began to ring from above.

"Wait here," said Brother Luca. "I'm going to the

chapter house." He hefted his book sack. "Soon as I hide my book somewhere, I'll be back."

He went off, leaving Bianca and me sitting on the low wall that ran along the canal at the far side of the campo. We watched as the friar hurried across the open space and then disappeared into the church.

"I like him," said Bianca.

"Glad he's our friend," I agreed.

For a moment, we just sat there. Thinking about my master, I was jittery but said nothing. Above, the dark sky began to clear. An almost-full moon kept popping out from stringy clouds, casting down a welcome white light. I saw a star.

"A long day," said Bianca.

"And not finished. We have to get to my master."

Bianca said, "Brother Luca will be back soon. If he doesn't help, we'll have to use your magic." She grimaced as she spoke, so I knew she didn't believe I had real magic.

"I wish I had some."

"You still must teach me tricks."

"Do you still have that coin?"

She handed it to me.

"Here's how to pull it out of somebody's nose."

I showed her how it was done, and she copied me. But as she practiced, I was getting increasingly impatient. Where was the friar?

As we continued to sit there, I said, "I know you have that prison key in your room, which will get us into the cells. But Brother Luca was right: How will we get my master *out* of the palazzo?"

"I'm not sure," she admitted. "Let's hope they brought him back to that same cell."

"Bianca . . ." I said after a few moments. "What if they killed my master?"

"We can pray not."

"Do people ever escape?"

"I've heard it's happened," she said. Then she added, "But not often."

I said, "I must get him back to Pergamontio."

"We'll find a way."

"But we'll need — Bianca, look," I cried, pointing across the campo. "It's them. Rozetti and Cardano."

CHAPTER 33

"WHERE?" SAID BIANCA.

"There," I said, jumping up. "By the church door. They're going into the church. We need to warn Brother Luca."

Bianca grabbed my arm. "If we do, they'll see us. Does he know what they look like?"

"I told him."

She continued to sit there, eyes fixed on the church. "He said he was going to the chapter house," she said. "At the back of the church, there's a new corner chapel. If we go that way, we can get inside the church and hopefully they won't see us." She was instantly up and running, me at her heels.

Upon reaching the end of the campo, Bianca turned and moved by some buildings that had nothing to do with the church. Then, with another shift, she ran along the church's side. I stayed with her.

"That's the chapel," she said, pointing to a small structure at the far end of the church. The doors being open, we rushed inside. A few people were there, kneeling in prayer before a glittering altar. Without pausing — no doubt a sin — Bianca turned right and exited the chapel by a side door, which gave us entry into the vast church itself at its far end.

Still running, we went across three more chapels and then the high altar. Without pausing — another sin — we went farther, into the sanctuary room, where we had gone that time with Brother Marco. As we did, Brother Luca emerged from an inside door.

"They're here," Bianca cried out.

The brother halted. "Who is?"

"Those assassins," I said. "Rozetti and Cardano. We saw them enter the church."

Without pause, Brother Luca turned, opened the door behind him, and said, "This way. Through the chapter house."

Bianca, remembering that the last time she had been forbidden entry, hesitated.

"Come, quickly," said the friar, beckoning.

Bianca and I rushed forward. Brother Luca led us into

a large hall, past the high writing table where the under-abbot had sat. Behind it were more long tables and benches. A few Franciscan brothers were sitting there, some eating, others reading. With the friar in the lead, we passed them at a run. Startled, priests looked up, but no one stopped us.

When we reached the far end of the hall, Brother Luca pushed open a side door and ushered us through. Once we were through, he pulled the door shut behind us. We were behind the church, in a dark alley.

"That way," he said, pointing toward the far end, where a lit lamp hung.

He ran, and we followed toward the lamp. Only when we stepped onto a small campo did we stop, panting for breath.

"Tell me again," said Brother Luca, "what did you see?"

I said, "Rozetti and Cardano."

"The ones who are after us?"

I nodded.

"They are persistent," said the brother.

"But . . ." said Bianca, "I'm pretty sure they didn't see us, and they don't know we're back here."

I looked around. "Where are we?"

"Not far from my room," said Bianca. "We can get my prison key."

"But they know about your room," I warned.

"They don't know we're going there."

"Can we get there fast?" asked Brother Luca. It was then that I realized he still had his leather satchel with him, which, I recalled, had held his book. I wanted to ask why he still had it, but there was no time.

"We'd better run," said Bianca, and she led us through and along the usual tangle of streets, alleys, and canals. It wasn't too long before I recognized that we were just beyond the entryway that led to Bianca's campo. Bending low, we hurried through, single file. Emerging at the other end, we found the campo empty. A bit of light came from a solitary candle lamp.

As we ran toward Bianca's room, I saw a sheet of paper had been stuck to her door. I also saw a large dangling lock. She must have seen them at the same moment because she plunged forward, ripped off the paper, and held it at a slant to capture enough light so she was able to read it.

When she did, she gasped, her face filling with a look of shock.

"It's . . . it's from the Galley Rowers Guild," she said, holding out the paper.

"What does it say?"

"My father's . . . my father's galley sank in a storm near Cyprus."

"Sank!"

She managed to nod.

"When?"

"Months ago. Everyone . . . was lost. And . . . and . . . I'm not allowed to use my room anymore."

I stared at her helplessly. I didn't know what to say. It was the friar, wiser than I, who dropped to his knees, wrapped his arms around Bianca, gathered her to his heart, and began to speak prayers. While she allowed this, she stood stiffly in his arms, even as tears flowed down her cheeks.

I just stood there until she reached a hand out toward me. When I took it, she drew me in, and as I went to my knees, the three of us clung to one another.

How hard it is, I thought, *to help someone who is grieving.*

I don't know how long we remained holding one another when, to my surprise, Bianca turned to me and said, "I don't want to let your master die, too."

With that, she tore away from Brother Luca, went to her door, and, as if in a fury, pushed hard against it, again and again. It wouldn't budge. "The lock," she said with despair.

Brother Luca threw his leather sack down and flung himself against the door, shoulder first. There was a loud thump, but the door refused to give way. He did it again, and that time I joined in. As did Bianca. It made no difference. The door remained shut.

"I need to sit," said Bianca, exhausted and out of breath. She walked to the well, slid to the ground, then sat with her back against it. Her eyes were closed, her hands clasped; tears glistened on her cheeks. Her breath was almost gulping while her face showed nothing but wretchedness.

I sat down beside her. "I'm sorry," I mumbled, angry at myself for not knowing how to say more. She made a slight shift of her body against me as if to tell me she accepted my words.

Brother Luca knelt before her, placing one of his hands on hers.

"Where is your mother?" he asked.

"Died."

"Brothers, sisters?"

"Died."

"Just Fabrizio here?"

"He's not really my brother. My godfather, Aswad, the gondolier, he's my only family. But you saw him. He's old and poor. He sleeps in his gondola."

"A convent," said Brother Luca. "The sisters will take you in."

"No," said Bianca with a vehement shake of her head and an angry twist to a strand of hair.

"We'll think of something," said the friar.

"I don't want to think about it," said Bianca. "I just want to think about Fabrizio's master. I don't want him to die, too. But my key is in that room."

Brother Luca said, "There must be other keys."

"The other one I know about is around Federico's neck."

"Who is Federico?" asked Brother Luca.

"The guard at the prison cells," I replied.

"Would he let us in?"

"I don't know," said Bianca. She smeared tears from her face. "Most times when I go there — at night — he's asleep. Fabrizio knows."

"We'll go in the morning," said the friar.

"No," insisted Bianca. "It has to be now, or we won't save Fabrizio's master." She held out her hand. I came to my feet and helped her stand.

"By gondola?" I asked.

"Aswad has done more than enough. We'll walk. Let's pray that Federico is asleep, or we won't be able to get in."

Without another word, she headed off, not looking to see if we were following. All but running, we left the campo, turned left, and kept going. I kept thinking how I could help her.

It wasn't long before we stepped out onto Piazza San Marco. Despite the late hour, as ever, many masked people were still there, illuminated by an almost-full moon that spread pale light over the many who were dancing to music. Perhaps they were celebrating the end of the storm. Or the coming end of carnival.

We weaved around the dancers and headed right to the Doges' Palazzo and that separate building at the end, the one with a sculpture of a man kneeling before a giant winged lion. Once there, we approached the flight of steps, which led to the palazzo's second level, lit by a wall lamp. As before, two soldiers were standing on guard. They were not the ones who had been there before, but they were dressed the same, with body armor and swords.

Bianca went right up to them. "Hey, Giovanni. Hey, Flavio," she called. "We have to go in."

"What's your business at this hour?"

She gestured to me. "This boy's father is to be executed in the morning." She gestured to Brother Luca. "We've come to pay our respects."

"A visit of mercy. All right. We can let you in. Step along. But be quick."

"Come on," Bianca said, and went up the steps. The

friar and I said nothing — though he raised his hand to bless the soldiers — and stayed right behind her.

She led us down the long balcony, passing the tall doors. Then she made the sharp turn that led to a hallway but halted at the open door.

"Where are we?" Brother Luca asked.

Bianca pointed. "The prison cells."

We continued, going up the steps until we saw that huge wooden door with heavy iron hinges. Sitting against the door at the top of the steps was Federico. As for his key, it was, as before, on a chain around his neck. But he was wide awake.

CHAPTER 34

"Ah, Bianca," Federico said with a smirk. "You're back."

She said, "We need to see a prisoner."

"Who?"

I said, "Mangus of Pergamontio."

"Who is that?"

"The magician."

Federico's eyes squinted. "Ah, yes. I've heard of him. Why should you care?"

Bianca turned to me for an answer. I didn't hesitate. "I'm his son."

"It's all one to me," said Federico. He turned to Bianca and held out his hand. "You know how it works. A paper from the authorities or —" He wiggled his fingers in the way the capitano on the galley had asked for money when we boarded his ship at Bari.

"I have no money," I said.

"Nor I," said Bianca.

Brother Luca said, "I can get some by tomorrow morning."

Federico shook his head. "Forgive me, Brother. That will be too late."

"Too late?" said Bianca. "Why?"

"He is to be executed at dawn."

It was all I had feared. I could hardly breathe.

"He's a magician," Federico went on. "Magic is illegal in the Serene Republic. And I suppose it's a sin as well," he added with a nod toward Brother Luca. "Still, I admit, I should have liked to have seen something of his sorcery."

Bianca said, "But surely the priest can see him."

"No one. By order of the Black Robes."

"Signor Cardano?" I said.

"Himself," said Federico with a nod.

The three of us stood there, Brother Luca holding his leather sack in his hand, Bianca staring at Federico. As for me, I didn't know what to do.

That's when Bianca said, "I can show you some magic."

"Can you?" said Federico, offering up a lopsided grin.

"Truly? I've never seen any. Since you are a magician's friend, I suppose you should know some. Go on. Do magic."

Bianca said, "You must not tell that Black Robe."

"Do I have the friar's absolution?" asked Federico.

Brother Luca raised his hand in a blessing. "You do."

"Good. All right, then, just between us," said Federico, and looked at Bianca.

She held out her hand toward Federico. "Give me that key you have hanging around your neck. I'll do something magical with it."

"What?"

"Just give me that key and you'll see."

"And you'll not tell anyone?"

"No one."

Fumbling, Federico pulled the key from the chain around his neck and handed it to Bianca. She took it, squeezed it into her left fist, made a pass with her right hand, rubbed both hands together, and opened her hand. The key had disappeared. In its place was a coin.

Federico's eyes goggled; his mouth hung open as he

stared at the coin. "How did you do that?" he cried with fright.

"Magic," she said. "Now I shall make you disappear."

"No," he cried, staggering to his feet. "Don't do that!"

"I will," she said, and lifted her hand.

Scared, he bolted past us, through the doorway, and down the passageway.

Brother Luca laughed. "Well done," he exclaimed.

"Perfect," I said, smiling.

Bianca inserted the key into the keyhole, turned it, and, with my help, shoved the door open. The three of us hurried down the hall, not pausing to investigate any of the cells until we reached the one where Mangus had been.

I peered in. Through the gloom, I saw two men were there. One was on the floor; the other was upon the low bed.

Bianca unlocked the cell door.

CHAPTER 35

I WENT RIGHT TO THE BED. TO MY RELIEF, IT WAS Mangus who lay there. In haste, I bent over him and listened to his ragged breathing.

I shook his arm gently. "Master," I said, not wishing to wake the other man, "I'm here to free you."

Mangus fluttered open his eyes and squinted at me. "Fabrizio? Is that you?"

"Yes, Master. With permission, you need to get up."

"Are they letting me go?"

"Best not to talk, Master," I said, keeping my voice low. "We need to hurry. I'll explain later."

Brother Luca and I helped Mangus get to his feet.

"Who is this?"

"Brother Luca Pacioli, Master."

"Truly?"

By this time, Brother Luca was opening his leather satchel. From it, he pulled some garments. "Here, Signore. Put these on. They will get you out." The clothing he had brought was a Franciscan robe, along with a white rope belt, and sandals.

Mangus made no resistance as we drew the robe around him. I set the hood over his head, pulling it low over his face. I also tied the white rope about his waist. Bianca put the sandals on his feet. Brother Luca adjusted his sleeves.

As we dressed him, Mangus said nothing.

"Come along, now," Brother Luca said, holding out his arm. Mangus took it. I was on his other side, holding his frail hand. As Bianca led the way, we guided him out of the cell.

We went back along the corridor. Federico had abandoned his post. At the bottom of the steps that led out of the palazzo, the guards had changed. What they saw were two Franciscan friars and two children descending the steps.

"What's going on here?" demanded a guard.

"We have merely brought comfort to an old prisoner," said Brother Luca. "Along with his grandchildren."

The guard studied us intently, as if trying to make up his mind.

I held my breath.

The guard moved aside.

I suppressed a grin even as I was thinking, *My family is getting bigger.*

As we went by the guards, Brother Luca said something in Latin to them and lifted his hand in a blessing. Then Brother Luca, Mangus, Bianca, and I stepped out onto the piazza.

Mangus was free.

We stood there, gazing about the crowded piazza.

Luca said: "If we're going to get completely away, I'm afraid we need to cross to the far side. Once there, I can arrange your escape."

I gazed over the swarming space. "With permission, Brother, I think I had better look around first," I said. "To make sure Rozetti and Cardano aren't about."

"A good idea," said the friar.

"But hurry," said Bianca. Then she, Brother Luca, and Mangus moved into a shadow along the side of the palazzo.

Leaving them, I ran forward, darting among the dancing people, musicians, and food sellers. With countless people in costume, or masked, and many moving about, I realized how difficult it would be to recognize anyone.

I don't know how long I wandered about until, with a combination of dread and relief, I saw Rozetti and Cardano at the far end of the piazza. They were wearing no masks but were walking about, doing, I realized, exactly what I was doing: searching.

Hoping they had not seen me, I spun about and raced to where Mangus, Bianca, and Brother Luca were waiting.

"They're on the piazza," I called out. "I'm sure they're looking for us."

"Did they see you?"

"I don't know. But they are coming this way."

Brother Luca said, "Behind the cathedral is the church and convent of Saint Zachariah. I know the sisters. I once helped them with their bookkeeping. I hope they'll remember. I'll ask them to give you sanctuary."

"Sanctuary?" I asked.

"It means the Church will protect you."

This time it was Brother Luca who guided us while Bianca and I supported Mangus, walking as fast as he was able. First, we went along the front of the cathedral, then along its side, to the back. From there, we passed over a canal via a small bridge, and farther, along a dark alleyway. I kept looking back but didn't see our enemies. As for Mangus, he said nothing. I continued to support him, trying to adjust our movement to his condition.

From the alley, we stepped onto a modest campo, at the head of which was a small church. A lit lamp illuminated its doorway framed by red-and-gray panels of stone.

"The Church and Convent of Saint Zachariah," said Brother Luca. "There's a very fine garden behind it. And the sisters are kind. Best of all, the church is under the particular protection of the doge, so it will be safe."

We went up to the door, upon which Brother Luca pounded.

The noise revived Mangus. He lifted his head. "Where are we?" he said.

"We're getting you to safety, Master."

"That friar is a good man."

"Brother Luca Pacioli at thy service, Signore."

"Have you given your bookkeeping method to my servant?"

"Servant? I thought he was your son."

"Close enough, Brother. But does he have the method?"

"Not yet, Signore."

For a moment, Mangus did not speak; then he said, "Fabrizio, either I'll die here, or if I go home without that method, I shall die there."

"I promise to ask, Master."

Mangus turned to Bianca. "You have been very kind."

"Thank you, Signore."

"Did Fabrizio tell you I was a magician?"

Bianca looked at me. I gave a tiny shake of my head.

"No, Signore," said Bianca. "Nothing of the sort."

"I'm not," said Mangus. "Fabrizio," he said in a plaintive voice, "you need to get me home."

"We'll get there, Master," I said, even as the church door opened.

A nun holding a candle was standing in the doorway. She was garbed in her long black habit, her wrinkled face framed by a white wimple. Her gray eyes studied us.

"Sister Francesca," said Brother Luca. "I pray you will remember me. Brother Luca. We must request sanctuary."

"I do remember you, Brother," said Sister Francesca. "And you're most welcome." She stepped back to make way for us. As soon as we went forward, the door — to my relief — was closed behind us.

The nun led us into a large room, empty save for a cross on one wall. There were several interior doors, all closed.

"We hold a room in readiness for those in distress," said Sister Francesca to Mangus, though I wasn't sure he understood. After indicating a door off to the side, the sister went and opened it, revealing a smaller room. There was a bed, a table, a chair, and a praying stool. No windows. On the wall hung a cross. There was also a painting that depicted Mary, the Infant, and Saint John the Baptist.

"You may remain here," said Sister Francesca as she handed her candle to Brother Luca. "How long will these people stay?"

"I need to make some arrangements," he replied. "We'll go as soon as possible."

"Food?"

"That would be appreciated."

"Fine," said the nun with a quick nod. She left, shutting the door behind her.

Bianca guided Mangus to the bed, where he lay down and closed his eyes. I covered him with the sole blanket that was there. He fell asleep at once. Bianca and I sat on the floor, near him.

To Brother Luca, I said, "My master is weak. He needs to get home."

"I will arrange things."

"With permission, Brother, can you tell me what that method is? I need to know."

"What method?"

"That bookkeeping secret."

He smiled. "Truly? Must you know now?"

"With permission. It's important. And if we are going . . ."

"I can try." He paused and then said, "When a business deal is made, somebody always *gets* something — that's called a debit. And something is *given* in return. That's called credit. That is the way business is done.

"The old way of accounting was with an abacus. You added and subtracted up and down in one row.

"The new bookkeeping method — which I explain in my book — is that each money deal is *equally* recorded in two or more columns on paper. When you spend money, you subtract the amount from your cash column and add the same amount to your expense column. The columns must balance. This allows merchants to better understand their business and to know whether they are earning or losing money. It's called double-entry bookkeeping."

That's when Bianca said, "That's what I do."

"You do?" I said, surprised.

"I told you," she said. "The merchants in the Rialto taught me how to keep my accounts. When I deliver things or messages to those prisoners," she explained, "they pay. Or sometimes I must buy things for them. They pay me back. I keep a record of it all. It's simple. When you paid me for my room, I wrote it down that way in my book."

"There you are," said Brother Luca with a smile.

Let me admit, I felt disappointed. I had wanted something magical. This was nothing of the kind. Moreover,

I thought of all that it took to learn this, and the folly of my efforts. And here Bianca knew it all along.

Brother Luca interrupted my thoughts. "Now I'll leave you and make arrangements for your departure." To Bianca, he said, "Your godfather, Aswad, that place where we came, is that where he lives?'

"In his gondola."

"I'll need to find him."

I asked, "How long will you be gone?"

"As briefly as possible. Those men may have followed you. It will be dangerous to leave this place. Remain here. Is that understood?"

"Yes, Brother."

"You have no money, do you?"

"None, Brother."

"I'll see what I can do about that, too. Now, again be patient."

With that, Brother Luca left us.

CHAPTER 36

MOMENTS LATER, SISTER FRANCESCA RETURNED with a wooden bowl of bread, cheese, and some dried meat. Mangus would not eat. But no sooner did the nun leave than Bianca and I devoured what had been brought.

As we sat, I asked Bianca, "With your room gone, where will you go?"

"I'm not sure."

"With Aswad?"

"He doesn't have a room. Just his gondola."

"You should come to Pergamontio. Master and Mistress are kind."

"Would they have me?"

"I'm sure they would. And you can explain that book-keeping method to our king."

She became quiet for a moment. Then she said, "I'd miss Venice."

"It is utterly different," I admitted.

"If I left, it would free Aswad to go home, which is what he wants. He can't look after me forever."

Not wanting to press her, we lapsed into silence.

Restless, still hungry, and unsure how to comfort her, I said, "Maybe I can get some more food."

I went out into the hall into which we had first come. It was empty. There were doors, but I was reluctant to open them.

As I had noticed before, this entry area had no windows. But as I looked about, I realized that the front door had a peephole that allowed one to see into the campo right before the church.

I looked through the hole. The moonlight allowed me to see two men sitting on a stone bench on the far side of the campo, facing the doorway. It took only a second for me to realize that it was Rozetti and Cardano. They must have seen me on the piazza and followed. No doubt they were now waiting for us to emerge.

My mind leaped to Brother Luca: *Does their waiting there mean they caught him?*

I hurried back to the room where Bianca was waiting, where Mangus still slept. "They are out there on the campo, waiting for us."

"Who is?"

"Rozetti and Cardano."

"Are you sure?"

"You can look for yourself. Bianca, we must get away."

"Where?"

"I don't know."

"But what about Brother Luca?"

"They might have captured him. And worse. Even if he's free, I'm not sure he'll be able to come back to us. We can't wait."

Bianca looked toward the sleeping Mangus. "Your master can't move. And we can't carry him."

"Do you think those men will come in here?"

"It's a convent. You heard Brother Luca: If they broke in, it would cause a scandal. If we stay here, we'll be safe."

"Then we'll have to wait here for Brother Luca, won't we?"

"Yes."

Which is what we did.

I tried to be patient, but it was painful for me to be

sitting while our enemies were right outside. What if Bother Luca had already been taken? We had no way of knowing.

We waited for what seemed a long time. Mangus continued to sleep. Restless, I don't know how long it was before I got up. "Where are you going?" Bianca asked.

"Maybe I can lure those men away. That way you and Mangus will be safe. Or you'll find some way to get away and hide."

"Fabrizio, don't be —"

I never heard the rest of her warning because I had already left the room, shutting the door behind me.

I went to the front door and peeked out again. Rozetti and Cardano were still lolling on the bench. Though they were waiting, they did not look alert.

I tried to reason: I needed to lead them away so we could remain safe. Also, once the two assassins were gone, Brother Luca could return — if he was still free.

But where to go? I had no true idea where we were, other than in the church, which was behind the piazza. Then I remembered something Brother Luca had said: that there was a fine garden behind the church.

My imaginings saw a garden thick with trees and shrubs. In other words, a place to hide. With that in mind, I formed a plan. I'd step out and allow myself to be seen by those men. Then I would lure them away from where they were by racing into that garden to hide. Once there, they would never find me.

I looked back at the door behind which Mangus and Bianca were waiting. I tried to decide if I should tell her what I was going to do. I had no doubt she'd tell me not to. Moreover, I told myself that if they caught me, it would be all right. At least she and Mangus would be able to get away. I owed her that for all my foolhardiness.

I looked out into the campo again. It now appeared as if Rozetti had fallen asleep — at least his head was bowed. That, I decided, gave me a better chance.

My first impulse was to slip out in secret. Then I reminded myself that I wanted them to see me so they would follow.

Boldly, I opened the door, stepped out, and stood there, trusting I'd be seen. Sure enough, Cardano jumped up and stared as if trying to make sure it was me.

"Rozetti," he said, waking his partner with a slap on his arm.

By then, I was already running across the campo — which is to say across the face of the church. When I reached the end, I raced along its side, along a dark lane. As I did, I saw a faint square of light ahead, what I presumed was the garden. As I rushed on, I heard running steps behind me. It was as I had hoped; they were coming after me.

I burst into what I anticipated would be a crowded garden, only to see just the opposite. The garden consisted of nothing but a few trimmed bushes, a solitary elm tree, and some lawn. In the center, the inevitable well made of white stone. Two buckets stood beside it, attached to the well's crossbar with rope. Moreover, a high, spiked wall ran along the rear of the garden, making it impossible to climb over. There was a door on that back wall, but I had no way of knowing if it was locked. And I didn't have time to check. Even as I stood there, running footsteps behind me were growing louder. There was only one place to hide: the well.

I ran to it and looked down. Moonlight allowed me to see water deep below. Frantic, I gripped one of the bucket ropes — one that was attached to the well's head bar — sat on the well's edge, dangled my feet into the hole, and pushed off, allowing myself to drop.

Down I fell, plunging into water up to my waist until my free fall was arrested as the rope, with a jerk, reached its limit. There, in desperation, I clung to the rope with two hands, dangling half-in, half-out of the water, knowing that if I let go, I would drown.

Even as I hung there, I heard voices from above.

"Where did he go?"

"Don't know. That wall is too high to get over."

"I told you; that boy is a magician," said another voice, which I recognized as Rozetti's. He swore a vile, blasphemous oath. "He makes things appear and disappear. Including himself. Though I put a curse on him in Pergamontio and laid a trap for him on the road to Bari, he got away. In Bari, he escaped from a locked room. You tried to dump him in a canal. That failed. We chased him. He escaped. He disappeared from that church on Torcello.

Now he's done it again. I tell you, the boy is a great magician, like his master. His magic is too strong for me."

"We should look some more."

"A waste of time. He'll just disappear again. I'm giving up."

"Don't worry. With that magician about to be executed, we just need to find the friar. We should go back to the Frari."

There were footsteps going away, and then silence. Needing to be absolutely certain they had gone, I continued to hang there a few more minutes.

The boy is a great magician. Rozetti's words echoed in my head and filled me with enormous pleasure.

The well was lined with rough brick. That allowed me — while pulling up, hand over hand, on the bucket rope — to walk up the side of the well, reach the top, swing over the edge, and drop down to the ground.

Once out of the well, I started back to Bianca, when I heard something behind me. I swung about just in time to see that back wall door swing open.

CHAPTER 37

Brother Luca stepped into the garden. As always, he had his leather satchel with him.

"Fabrizio," he called. "What are you doing here?"

"Making our enemies disappear," I said.

"What are you talking about?"

I told him what I had done.

"Well done. It takes a brave man to know when to hide. But where is Bianca? Where is your master?"

"In the church."

"We need to fetch them. I've managed to find a boat that will get you to Bari. All we have to do is get to where it's moored on the other side of the piazza."

We went back into the church and got Mangus up. I told them what I had done, which made Bianca laugh, the first time I had seen her ever do that.

It was then that Pacioli reached into his leather satchel and pulled out two masks. Made of stiff paper, one was painted to look like a dog's face. The other looked like the head of a green fish.

“Put them on,” Brother Luca urged Bianca and me.

She took the dog head. I took the fish. The brother fastened them around our heads with string.

“Now,” he announced, “we are two friars with our young wards celebrating carnival.”

We started off, but as we passed the entryway to the palazzo, Brother Luca stopped. From his satchel, he pulled out a paper and handed it to me. “I have drawn up a denunciation of Rozetti and Cardano and signed my name on it. Go, put it in the lion’s mouth.”

More than happy to do so, I raced up to the lion and stuffed the paper into the mouth and returned to my friends.

We then headed across the piazza — albeit slowly — but thankfully, no one took notice of us.

When we reached the banks of the Grand Canal, there was a topo, a single-masted sailing fishing boat, the kind that Rozetti had used to chase us to Torcello. Brother Luca had managed to rent one. What’s more, to Bianca’s great delight, it was Aswad who was at the helm.

We helped Mangus walk to it and got him aboard.

“It stinks of fish” was his comment.

"Better the stink of fish than the stink of death," said Brother Luca.

"I'll sail you to Bari," said Aswad. "With good winds, it should take us only two days."

"And here," said Brother Luca, "is money enough to get you home."

I turned to him. "A million, million thanks, Brother. But with permission, what will you do?"

"I need to finish the work on my book. Once I fetch it back from the Frari — and you may be sure I'll be careful — there are many churches in Venice where I can hide from those men if they are still pursuing me. But our denunciation should catch them up. You need not worry."

It was then I turned to Bianca. "Will you come with us?" I asked.

"Will your master and mistress truly take me in?"

"I promise."

She turned to Brother Luca. "I must ask a favor."

"Which is?"

"The people in the prisons depend on me to bring food and messages that their friends and family send them. Will you find someone to do that?"

"I'm sure I can."

She handed him the prison key. To me, she said, "I'll go with you."

Then, just about when we were set to go, Brother Luca said, "I almost forgot." He handed me a sheaf of papers.

"Here," he said, "is *The Rules of Double-Entry Bookkeeping*. My printer will be able to make another copy of my manuscript. You may give that to your king. I'm happy to share my knowledge with the world."

We made our farewells and gave heartfelt thanks. Brother Luca blessed us. The last I saw of him was when he disappeared amid the crowds on Piazza San Marco.

Our voyage down the sea to Bari, although somewhat cold and uncomfortable, proved easy. The sea air, acceptable food, and knowing we were going home revived Mangus's spirits and helped him regain strength moment by moment.

When we reached Bari, Bianca and Aswad went off a bit on their own. From the way they held each other, I could see they were making their farewells.

They were long and, I suspect, tearful exchanges, with cheeks kissed and hugs exchanged. I had no doubt she was promising that she would soon return to him in Venice, while he vowed the same after seeing his family in Egypt. But from the pain I saw on their faces, I suspected both knew it would not happen.

Then Aswad went off.

With the money Brother Luca had given us, we three stayed one night in Bari at the Safe Harbor, where I collected our possessions. I did purchase a new donkey, making sure it was one with a cross on his back. Thus, we made our way back to Pergamontio without any incident.

As you might imagine, Mistress Sophia received us with boundless joy. When I introduced Bianca and told her she was my "long-lost sister," the girl was welcomed into our house, with embraces and many kisses on her cheeks.

Though embarrassed, I saw that Bianca was pleased.

The next day, we — Mangus, Bianca, and I — made our way up to the Castello. When we put in our names, we were granted an audience with King Claudio.

He was sitting on his golden throne. Mangus

approached and offered up the papers Pacioli had given us.

"My lord, here is the book you requested, Friar Luca Pacioli's bookkeeping method."

The king flipped through the pages. The look on his face was bewilderment. "But can you explain it all?"

"Bianca can," said Mangus.

At which point, Bianca stepped forward and explained the accounting method in detail.

King Claudio acted satisfied.

"Have you news of Signor Rozetti?" asked the king. "Against my wishes, he appears to have followed you to Venice."

"My lord, we saw him there," said Mangus. "He must have been detained."

"Then he shall not have a position with me anymore. I hereby banish him from Pergamontio — if he ever shows up."

As we left the throne room, Bianca whispered to me, "He only pretended to understand the bookkeeping method. He'll not be able to use it."

I laughed and said, "But he'll never admit it."

That night, while we had our family meal, Mangus lifted his glass and gave a toast: "Happy is he who can return to his home. Blessed be my wife. Thanks to Fabrizio — a true son — who managed all with wonderful skill. Welcome to Bianca, who did much to save us and has made our family better."

And indeed, when the table was cleared, Bianca leaned over and said into my ear, "I think I'll like it here."

In the late evening, when Bianca had been given her own room, and Master and Mistress had retired, I climbed up to my attic space. Once on my straw bed, I thought of the things I had been told about Venice. That it was an island, with no roads, only canals. That to get there, one needed to have a boat with legs. That the city was full of winged lions. That people wore masks. That the way you dealt with criminals was to stuff them into the mouths of lions.

As I thought about it, I realized it was all true, in a fashion.

I retrieved Brother Pacioli's book: *On the Power of Numbers*. I turned to the section about magic and began to read. Even as I did, the cathedral bells began to ring the midnight hour.

I went back to Brother Luca Pacioli's book. It wasn't long before I was telling myself: *I can learn these tricks.*

AUTHOR'S NOTE

Luca Pacioli (1447–1517) was an Italian mathematician at a time when mathematics was considered part of philosophy. A Franciscan friar, and the leading Renaissance mathematician of his day, his most famous work was the *Summa de arithmetica*, an encyclopedia of all (in his day) known mathematics. One chapter described, for the first time, double-entry bookkeeping. That chapter has been called "the most important work in the development of capitalism." The accounting rules he set down spread around the world and soon became the international business standard, still in use to this day.

Pacioli was a close friend and collaborator of Leonardo da Vinci and wrote important books on proportion (with Da Vinci). It is believed he helped Da Vinci design the painting *The Last Supper.*

Pacioli also wrote an early book on chess, though it was not published, as well as the first European book that contained magic tricks. It was called *On the Power of Numbers.*

In my tale, some of the actual dates of Pacioli's publications have been shifted for the sake of the story. But he did write such books.